KU-015-462

Wildfire Island Docs

Welcome to Paradise!

Meet the small but dedicated team of medics
who service the remote Pacific Wildfire Island.

In this idyllic setting relationships are rekindled,
passions are stirred, and bonds that will last a lifetime
are forged in the tropical heat...

But there's also a darker side to paradise—secrets, lies and
greed amidst the Lockhart family threaten the community,
and the team find themselves fighting to save more than
the lives of their patients. They must band together to fight
for the future of the island they've all come to call home!

Dear Reader,

This is the sixth romance in the Wildfire Island Docs series, and it marks the end of one of the most dramatic, exotic series I've ever been involved in. Wildfire Island is a tropical paradise. Our heroes and heroines are our ideal lovers, the most skilled, the most gorgeous and the most fun doctors, nurses and paramedics... Oh, and did I mention the most sexy?

Meredith Webber, Alison Roberts and I have loved co-creating our characters, our worlds, our romances. Each is a stand-alone love story, but together we believe they're awesome. Linked stories push our creative boundaries, and they deepen our friendship in the process.

Max and Hettie's story tugged on my heartstrings as I wrote it, and I hope you'll be as touched by it as I've been. I love how much they deserve their happy ending. Let me know if you enjoy it—write to me at marion@marionlennox.com. If you love it as much as we do...who knows? We may be recruiting more medics for Wildfire!

Meanwhile, happy reading.

Marion

A CHILD TO OPEN THEIR HEARTS

BY
MARION LENNOX

Published in Great Britain 2016
By Mills & Boon, an imprint of HarperCollins*Publishers*
1 London Bridge Street, London, SE1 9GF

© 2016 Marion Lennox

ISBN: 978-0-263-26407-4

Our policy is to use papers that are natural, renewable and recyclable
products and made from wood grown in sustainable forests. The logging
and manufacturing processes conform to the legal environmental
regulations of the country of origin.

Printed and bound in Great Britain
by CPI Antony Rowe, Chippenham, Wiltshire

Marion Lennox has written over a hundred romance novels, and is published in over a hundred countries and thirty languages. Her international awards include the prestigious RITA® award (twice) and the *RT Book Reviews* Career Achievement award for 'a body of work which makes us laugh and teaches us about love'. Marion adores her family, her kayak, her dog, and lying on the beach with a book someone else has written. Heaven!

Books by Marion Lennox

Mills & Boon Medical Romance

The Surgeon's Doorstep Baby
Miracle on Kaimotu Island
Gold Coast Angels: A Doctor's Redemption
Waves of Temptation
A Secret Shared...
Meant-to-Be Family
From Christmas to Forever?
Saving Maddie's Baby

Mills & Boon Cherish

A Bride for the Maverick Millionaire
Sparks Fly with the Billionaire
Christmas at the Castle
Nine Months to Change His Life
Christmas Where They Belong

Visit the Author Profile page
at millsandboon.co.uk for more titles.

My books in this series are dedicated to Andy, whose help and friendship during my writing career has been beyond measure. I've been so proud to call you my friend.

CHAPTER ONE

THIS COULD BE a disaster instead of a homecoming. He could be marooned at sea until after his daughter's wedding.

Max wasn't worrying yet, though. Things would be chaotic on Wildfire Island after the cyclone, but the weather had eased and Sunset Beach was a favourite place for the locals to walk. If the rip wasn't so fierce he could swim ashore. He couldn't, but eventually someone would stroll to the beach, see his battered boat and send out a dinghy.

Max Lockhart, specialist surgeon, not-so-specialist sailor, headed below deck and fetched himself a beer. There were worse places to be stuck, he conceded. The *Lillyanna* was a sturdy thirty-foot yacht, and she wasn't badly enough damaged to be uncomfortable. She was now moored in the tropical waters off Wildfire Island. Schools of tiny fish glinted silver as they broke the surface of the sparkling water. The sun was warm. He had provisions for another week, and in the lee of the island the sea was relatively calm.

But he *was* stuck. The waters around the island were still a maelstrom. The cliffs that formed the headland above where he sheltered were being battered. To try and round them to get to Wildfire Island's harbour would be suicidal, and at some time during the worst of the cyclone his radio had been damaged and his phone lost overboard.

So now he was forced to rest, but rest, he conceded, had been the whole idea of sailing here. He needed to take some time to get his head in order and ready himself to face the islanders.

He also needed space to come to terms with anger and with grief. How to face his daughter's wedding with joy when he was so loaded with guilt and sadness he couldn't get past it?

But rest wouldn't cut it, he decided as he finished his beer. What he needed was distraction.

And suddenly he had it. Suddenly he could see two people on the island.

A woman had emerged from the undergrowth and was walking a dog on the beach. And up on the headland…another woman was walking towards the cliff edge.

Towards the cliff edge? What the…?

As a kid, Max and his mates had dived off this headland but they'd only dived when the water had been calm. They'd dared each other to dive the thirty-foot drop. Then they'd let the rip tug them out to this reef, where they'd catch their breath for the hard swim back. It had kept them happy for hours. It had given their parents nightmares.

For the woman on the headland, though, the nightmare seemed real. She was walking steadily towards the edge.

Suicide? The word slammed into his head and stayed.

He grabbed his field glasses, one of the few things not smashed in the storm, and fought to get them focussed. The woman was young. A crimson shawl was wrapped around a bundle at her breast. A child?

She was walking purposefully forward, closer to the edge. After the cyclone, the water below was a mass of churning foam. Even as a kid he'd known he had to get a run up to clear the rocks below.

'No!' His yell would be drowned in the wind up there, but he yelled anyway. 'Don't...'

His yell was useless. She reached the cliff edge and walked straight over.

Hettie de Lacey, charge nurse of Wildfire Island's small hospital, rather enjoyed a good storm. It broke the humidity. It cleared the water in the island's lagoons and it made the world seem fresh and new.

This, however, had been more than a good storm. The cyclone had smashed across the island three days ago, causing multiple casualties. Even though most wounds had been minor, the hospital was full to bursting, and Hettie had been run off her feet.

This was the first time she'd managed a walk and some blessed time to herself. Sunset Beach was relatively sheltered, but she was close to the northern tip, where waves flung hard against the headland. The seas out there were huge.

In another life she might have grabbed a surfboard and headed out, she thought, allowing herself a whiff of memory, of an eighteen-year-old Hettie in love with everything to do with the sea.

Including Darryn...

Yeah, well, that was one memory to put aside. How one man could take such a naïve kid and smash her ideals... Smash her life...

'Get over it,' she told herself, and she even smiled at the idea that she should still angst over memories from all those years ago. She'd made herself a great life. She was... mostly happy.

And then her attention was caught.

There was a yacht just beyond the reef. It was a gracious old lady of a yacht, a wooden classic, anchored to the south of The Bird's Nest. The Nest was a narrow rim of rock and coral, a tiny atoll at the end of an underwater reef running out from shore.

The yacht was using the atoll for shelter.

It'd be Max Lockhart, she thought, and the nub of fear she'd been feeling for Caroline dissipated in an instant. Oh, thank heaven. She knew the owner of Wildfire Island was trying to sail here for his daughter's wedding. Max had left Cairns before the cyclone had blown up, and for the last few days Caroline Lockhart, one of Hettie's best nurses, had been frantic. Her father was somewhere out to sea. He'd lost contact three days ago and they had no way of knowing if he'd survived.

She could see him fairly clearly from where she was, but she'd never met him—his few visits to the island during her employment had always seemed to coincide with times when she'd taken leave. But this must be him. The entrance to the harbour was wild so this was probably the safest place he could be.

She went to wave, and then she hesitated. The guy on the yacht—it must be Max—was already waving. And yelling. But not at her. At someone up on the headland?

Intrigued, she headed to the water's edge and looked up. Another islander out for a walk? Max must be stuck, she thought. He'd be wanting to attract attention so someone could send a dinghy out to bring him in. He'd seen someone up on the cliffs?

And then her breath caught in horror. Where the shallows gave way to deep water and the cliffs rose steeply to the headland, the wind still swept in from the cyclone-ravaged sea.

And up on the headland… Sefina Dason.

The woman was thirty feet above her but Hettie would know her anywhere. For the last few days Sefina had been in hospital, battered, not by the cyclone but by her oaf of a husband. She'd had to bring her toddler in with her because no one would care for him, something almost unheard of in this close-knit community.

There'd been whispers...

But this wasn't the time for whispers. Sefina was high on the headland and she was walking with purpose.

She was headed for the edge of the cliff!

And then she turned, just a little, and Hettie saw a bundle, cradled to her breast in a crimson shawl. Her horror doubled, trebled, went off the scale.

Joni!

No! She was screaming, running, stumbling over the rocks as beach gave way to the edges of the reef. *No!*

She could hear the echoes of the guy on the yacht, yelling, too.

But yelling was useless.

Sefina took two steps forward and she was gone.

Max knew the water under the headland like the back of his hand. In good weather this was a calm, still pool, deep and mysterious, bottoming out to coral. It was a fabulous place for kids to hurl themselves off the cliff in a show of bravado. The rip swept in from the north, hit the pool and tugged the divers out to the rocky outcrop he was anchored behind. As kids they'd learned to ride the rip to their advantage, letting it pull them across the shallow reef to the atoll. They'd lie on the rocks and catch their breath, readying themselves for the swim across the rip back to the beach.

But that rip would be fierce today, too strong to swim against. And the water in the pool...would be a whirlpool, he thought, sucking everything down.

All this he thought almost instantly, and as he thought it he was already tearing up the anchor, operating the winch with one hand, gunning the engine with the other.

His mind seemed to be frozen, but instinct was kicking in to take over.

Where would she be hurled out?

He hit the tiller and pushed the throttle to full speed, heading out of the shelter of the atoll, steering the boat as close as he dared to the beach. He couldn't get too close. Sheltered or not, there were still breakers pounding the sand.

There was a woman running along the beach, screaming. The woman with the dog? She'd seen?

But he didn't have time to look at her. He was staring across the maelstrom of white water, waiting for something to emerge. Anything.

He was as close as he could get without wrecking the yacht. As far as he could tell, this was where the rip emerged.

He dropped anchor, knowing he'd be anchoring in sand, knowing there was a chance the boat would be dragged away, but he didn't have time to care.

There… A wisp of crimson cloth… Nothing more, but it had to be enough.

If he was right, she was being tugged to twenty feet forward of the boat.

He'd miss her…

He was ripping his clothes off, tearing. Clothes would drag him down. If he used a lifejacket he could never swim fast enough.

He had so little chance the thing was almost futile.

He saw the wisp of crimson again, and he dived.

Sefina.

Joni.

Hettie was screaming but she was screaming inside. She had no room for anything else. Where…?

She'd swum here. There was a rip, running south. Hettie could swim well. Surfing had once been her life, but to swim against the rip in these conditions…

The guy on the boat had seen. If she could grab Sefina and tow her with the rip, maybe he could help.

A mother and a toddler?

She couldn't think like that.

As a teenager she'd trained as a lifeguard, hoping for a holiday job back when she'd lived at Bondi. Her instructor's voice slammed back now. *'Look to your own safety before you look to help someone in the surf.'*

This was crazy. Past dangerous.

Oh, but Joni… He was fifteen months old and she'd cradled him to sleep for the past few nights. And Sefina… Battered Sefina, with no one to turn to.

Forget the instructors. Her clothes were tossed onto the sand. 'Stay,' she yelled at Bugsy, and she was running into the waves regardless.

The rip was so strong Max was swept south the moment he hit the water. Anything in that pool would be tugged straight out, past the reef and out to sea.

He surfaced, already being pulled.

But Max had swum like a fish as a kid, and for the past few years gym work and swimming had sometimes seemed the only thing that had kept him sane.

He couldn't swim against the rip but if he headed diagonally across he might collide with…with what he hoped to find. That slip of crimson.

He cast one long look at the pool, trying to judge where he'd last seen that flash of crimson.

He put his head down and swam.

Was she nuts? Trying to swim in this surf? But if she got past the breakers she only had the rip to contend with. She could deal with the rip, she thought. She knew enough not to panic. The guy on the boat would have seen her. If she could reach Sefina and hold on to her, she could tread water until help came.

Even if the guy hadn't seen her, she was due to go on duty at midday. The staff knew she'd gone for a walk on the beach. If she didn't return they'd come down and find Bugsy, find her clothes… Once the rip dragged her out, she could tread water and hope…

Yeah, very safe, she thought grimly as she dived through another wave. *Not.*

What would she do if she reached them? The lifeguard part of her was already playing out scenarios.

The quickest way to kill yourself is to put yourself within reach of someone who's drowning. They'll pull you down as they try to save themselves.

There was her instructor again.

Sefina wouldn't try to save herself, though. Sefina wanted to die.

Sefina…

She'd known how unhappy the girl was, but in the post-cyclone chaos all Hettie had been able to give the young woman had been swift hugs between periods of impera-tive medical need. She'd promised her she was safe in the hospital. She'd promised they'd sort things out when things had settled.

She hadn't realised time had been so achingly short.

Hettie surfaced from the last breaker and looked around wildly. The rip was stronger than she'd thought. Maybe she'd missed them.

And then she saw someone else in the water, swimming strongly across the rip. The guy from the boat?

There went her source of help if she got into trouble, she thought grimly. All of them in the water? This was breaking every lifesaving rule, but it was too late to back out now. She was watching the rim of the foam where the deep pool ended and the relative calm began.

There! A sliver of crimson.

She must have shouted because the swimming guy raised his head. She waved and pointed.

He raised a hand in silent acknowledgement and they both put their heads down and swam.

He could see her now, or he could see the swirl of crimson shawl she'd wrapped around her body. If he could just get closer...

The pull of the rip was hauling him backwards. By rights it should've propelled the woman's body towards him.

Was she stuck on the edge of the reef? Had the shawl snagged?

The rocks were too close to the surface for safety. He should stay well clear...

He didn't.

This was crazy. Suicidal. She couldn't swim into the foam. She daren't. As it was, the rip was pulling so hard she was starting to doubt her ability to get herself to safety.

A breaker crashed on the rocks and threw a spray of water, blocking her vision. She could see nothing.

With a sob of fear and frustration she stopped trying and let herself be carried outward.

Free from the foam she could tread water. She could look again.

She could see nothing but white. Nothing...

There! Max's hands had been groping blindly in front of him, but the touch of fabric had him grabbing.

He had her, but she was wedged in rocks. He was being washed by breaker after breaker. He couldn't see. He pulled upwards to take a tighter hold—and a child fell free into his arms.

The child must have been clinging, or tied within the shawl. The rip caught them again and they were tugged outwards.

He had a child in his arms. He had no choice but to let himself go. To ride the rip…

He was pushing the child up, rolling onto his back, trying to get the little one into the air. The water was sweeping…

'Here!'

It was a yell and suddenly someone was beside him. A woman, dark-haired, fierce.

'Give him to me. Help Sefina. Please!'

'You can't hold him.' He didn't even know if the child was alive.

Her face was suddenly inches from his, soaking curls plastered across her eyes, green eyes flashing determination. 'I can. I know what to do. Trust me.'

And what was there in that that made him believe her?

What was there in that that made him thrust the limp little body into her arms and turn once again towards the rocks?

He had to trust her. He had to hope.

Joni was breathing. He'd been limp when he'd been thrust at her, but as she rolled and prepared to breathe for him—yes, she could do it in the water; lifesaver training had been useful—the little one gasped and choked and gasped again.

His eyes were shut, as if he'd simply closed down, ready for death. How many children drowned like this? Thirteen years as a nurse had taught Hettie that when children slipped untended into water they didn't struggle. They drowned silently.

Somehow, though, despite not fighting, Joni must have

breathed enough air to survive. As she touched his mouth with her lips he gasped and opened his eyes.

'Joni.' She managed to get his name out, even though she was fighting for breath herself. 'It's okay. Let's get you to the beach.'

His huge brown eyes stared upwards wildly. Joni was fifteen months old, a chubby toddler with beautiful coffee-coloured skin and a tangle of dark curls. He was part islander, part...

Well, that was the problem, Hettie thought, her heart clenching in fear for his mother.

She couldn't do anything for Sefina, though. The sailor—Max?—had handed her Joni and she had to care for him.

Where was he now? she wondered as she trod water. Her first impressions had been of strength, determination, resolution. His face had been almost impassive.

He'd need strength and more if he was swimming back against the reef. The risks...

She couldn't think of him now. Her attention had to be on keeping Joni safe.

Keeping them both safe?

She cupped her hand around Joni's chin and started side-stroking, as hard and fast as she could, willing him to stay limp. The rip was still a problem. Getting back to the beach was impossible. The boat was too close to the breakers, but the atoll at the end of the reef might just be possible. If she could just reach the rocks...

Blessedly Joni stayed limp. *It must be shock*, she thought as she fought the current, but she was thankful for it. He lay still while she towed.

But the rip was strong. She was fighting for breath herself, kicking, using every last scrap of strength she had, but she couldn't do it. She couldn't reach the atoll. It was so near and yet so far.

If she could just keep floating, someone would help, she thought. If she rode the rip out, if she could hold on to Joni...

But if he struggled...

She had no choice. The rip was too strong to fight.

She held him as far out of the water as she could and let herself be carried out to sea.

He had her. For what it was worth, he had her, but she was dead. He could see the head injury. He could see the way her head floated limply.

She must have crashed onto the rocks, he thought. She'd stepped straight down instead of diving outwards. Death would have been instantaneous. It had been a miracle that the child had stayed with her.

He had her free of the reef, but what to do now? He couldn't get her to the beach. There was no way he could fight the rip. It was carrying them out fast, towards the atoll. Did he have enough strength to get them both there?

By himself there'd be no problem, but holding this woman...

He couldn't.

She was dead. Let her go.

He couldn't do that, either. A part of him was still standing at his son's gravesite.

A part of him was remembering burying his wife, all those years ago.

Somewhere, someone loved this woman. To not have a chance to say goodbye... It would have killed him.

Holding on to her might kill him. He couldn't keep fighting for both of them.

Despite the strength of the rip, the water he was in was relatively calm. He was fighting to get across the current but he paused for a moment in his fight to get a bearing. To see...

And what he saw made him rethink everything. The woman he'd given the child to still held him, but they were drifting fast, so fast they'd miss the atoll. They were being pulled to the open sea.

The woman didn't seem to be panicking. She had the child in the classic lifesaver hold. She seemed to know her stuff, but she wasn't strong enough. In minutes she'd be past the atoll and she'd be gone.

A woman and a child, struggling for life.

A woman in his arms, for whom life was over.

Triage. Blessedly it slammed back. For just a moment he was a junior doctor again in an emergency room, faced with the decision of which patient to treat first.

No choice.

He gave himself a fraction of a second, a moment where he tugged the woman's body around and faced her. He memorised everything about her so he could describe her, and then, in an aching, tearing gesture that seemed to rip something deep inside, he touched her face. It was a gesture of blessing, a gesture of farewell.

It was all he could do.

He let her go.

She'd never reach it. Her legs simply weren't strong enough to kick against the current.

She was so near and yet so far. She was being pulled within thirty yards of the atoll and yet she didn't have the strength to fight.

If she was swept out… If Max didn't make it… How long before they could expect help?

The child in her arms twisted unexpectedly and she almost lost him. She fought for a stronger hold but suddenly he was fighting her.

'Joni, hush. Joni, stay still…'

But he wasn't listening, wasn't hearing. Who knew what he was thinking?

She was being swept…

And then, blessedly, she was being grabbed herself by the shoulders from behind. She was being held with the swift, sure strength of someone who'd been trained, who knew how to gain control.

Max?

'Let me take him.' It was an order, a curt command that brooked no opposition. 'Get yourself to the atoll.'

'You can't.'

'You're done,' he said, and she knew she was.

'S-Sefina?'

'She's dead. We can't do anything for her. Go. I'm right behind you.'

And Joni was taken from her arms.

Relieving her of her load should have made her lighter. Free. Instead, stupidly, she wanted to sink. She hadn't known how exhausted she was until the load had been lifted.

'Swim,' Max yelled. 'We haven't done this for nothing. Swim, damn you, now.'

She swam.

He could do this. He would do this.

Too many deaths…

It was three short weeks since he'd buried his son. The waste was all around him, and the anger.

Maybe it was Christopher who gave him strength. Who knew?

'Keep still,' he growled, as the little boy struggled. There was no time for reassurance. No time for comfort. But it seemed to work.

The little boy subsided. His body seemed to go limp but

he reached up and tucked a fist against Max's throat. As if checking his pulse?

'Yeah, I'm alive,' Max muttered grimly, as he started kicking again against the rip. 'And so are you. Let's keep it that way.'

Rocks. The atoll was tiny but she'd made it. The last few yards across the rip had taken every ounce of her strength, but she'd done it.

She'd had to do it. If Max and Joni were swept out, someone had to raise the alarm.

She wasn't in any position to raise any alarm right now. It was as much as she could do to climb onto the rocks.

She knew this place. She'd swum out here in good weather. She knew the footholds but her legs didn't want to work. They'd turned to jelly, but somehow she made them push her up the few short steps to the relatively flat rock that formed the atoll's tiny plateau.

Then she sank to her knees.

She wanted—quite badly—to be sick, but she fought it down with a fierceness born of desperation. How many times in an emergency room had she felt this same appalling gut-wrench, at waste, at loss of life, at life-changing injuries? But her training had taught her not to faint, not to throw up, until after a crisis was past. Until she wasn't needed.

There was a crisis now, but what could she do? She wasn't in an emergency room. She wasn't being a professional.

She was sitting on a tiny rocky outcrop, while out there a sailor fought for a toddler's life.

Was he Max Lockhart?

More importantly, desperately more importantly, where was he? She hadn't been able to look back while she'd fought to get here, but now...

Max…Joni…

She was a strong swimmer but she hadn't been able to fight the rip.

Please… She was saying it over and over, pleading with whomever was prepared to listen. For Joni. For the unknown guy who was risking his life…

Was he Max? Father of Caroline? Owner of this entire island?

Max Lockhart, come home to claim his rightful heritage?

Max Lockhart, risking his life to save one of the islanders who scorned him?

So much pain…

If he died now, how could she explain it to Caroline? For the last three days, when the cyclone had veered savagely and unexpectedly across the path of any boat making its way here from Cairns, Hettie's fellow nurse had lost contact with her father. She'd been going crazy.

How could she tell her he'd been so near, and was now lost? With the child?

Or not. She'd been staring east, thinking that, if anything, he'd be riding the rip, but suddenly she saw him. He was south of the atoll. He must have been swept past but somehow managed to get himself out of the rip's pull. Now he was stroking the last few yards to the rocks.

He still had Joni.

She'd been out of the water now for five minutes. She had her breath back. Blessedly, she could help. She clambered down over the rocks, heading out into the shallows, reaching for Joni.

She had him. They had him.

Safe?

CHAPTER TWO

FOR A WHILE they were too exhausted to speak. They were too exhausted to do anything but lie on the rocks, Joni somehow safe between them.

The little boy was silent, passive...past shock? Maybe she was, too, and as she looked at Max collapsed beside them she thought, *That makes three.*

'S-Sefina,' she whispered.

'Neck,' he managed, and it was enough to tell her what she needed to know.

Oh, God, she should have...

Should have what? Cradled Sefina yesterday as she was cradling Joni now?

Yes, if that's what it would have taken.

If this had happened at a normal time... But it hadn't. Sefina had been admitted into hospital, bashed almost to the point of death, while the cyclone had been building. With the cyclone bearing down on them Hettie hadn't had time to do more than tend to the girl's physical needs.

Afterwards, when there'd been time to take stock and question her, Keanu, the island doctor on duty, had contacted the police. 'I want her husband brought in. With the extent of these injuries it's lucky he didn't kill her.'

It's lucky he didn't kill her...

She remembered Keanu's words and her breath caught on a sob.

Hettie de Lacey was a professional. She didn't cry. She held herself to herself. She coped with any type of trauma her job threw at her.

But she sobbed now, just once, a great heaving gulp that shook her entire body. And then somehow she pulled herself back together. Almost.

Max's arm came over her, over Joni, enfolding them both, and she needed it. She needed his touch.

'You're safe,' he told her. 'And the little one's safe.' And then he added, 'Keep it together. For now, we're all he has.'

It was a reminder. It wasn't a rebuke, though. It was just a fact. She'd been terrified, she was shocked and exhausted, and she still had to come to terms with what had happened, but the child between them had to come first.

And Max himself… He'd swum over those rocks. Over that coral…

She took a couple of deep breaths and managed to sit up. The sun was full out. The storm of the past days was almost gone. Apart from the spray blasting the headland and the massive breakers heading for shore, this could be just a normal day in paradise.

Wildfire Island. The M'Langi isles. This was surely one of the most beautiful places in the world.

The world would somehow settle.

She gathered Joni into her arms and held him tight, crooning softly into his wet curls. He was still wearing a sodden hospital-issue nappy and a T-shirt one of the nurses had found for him in the emergency supplies. It read, incongruously, 'My grandma went to London and all she brought me back was this T-shirt'.

It was totally inappropriate. Joni didn't have a grandma, or not one who'd acknowledge him.

Max had allowed himself a couple of moments of lying

full length in the sun, as if he needed its warmth. Of course he did. They all did. But now he, too, pushed himself to sitting, and for the first time she saw his legs.

They'd been slashed on the coral. He had grazes running from groin to toe, as if the sea had dragged him straight across the rocks.

What cost, to try and save Sefina?

He'd saved Joni.

'I never could have got him here,' she whispered, still holding him tight. The toddler was curled into her, as if her body was his only protection from the outside world. 'I never could have saved him without you.'

'Do you know…? Do you know who he is?' Max asked.

'His name is Joni Dason. His mother's name is…was Sefina.'

'A friend?' He was watching her face. 'She was your friend?'

'I… A patient.' And then she hesitated. 'But I was present at Joni's birth. Maybe I was…Sefina's friend. Maybe I'm the only…'

And then she stopped. She couldn't go on.

'I'm Max Lockhart,' Max said, and she managed to nod, grateful to be deflected back to his business rather than having to dwell on her shock and grief.

'I guessed as much when I saw your yacht. Caroline will be so relieved. She's been out of her mind with worry.'

'My boat rolled. I lost my radio and phone three days ago. Everything that could be damaged by water was damaged.'

'So you've been sitting out here, waiting for someone to notice you?'

'I reached the island last night. It was too risky to try for the harbour, and frankly I wasn't going to push my luck heading to one of the outer islands. So, yes, I've been here overnight but no one's noticed.'

'I noticed.'

'Thank you. You are?'

'Hettie de Lacey. Charge nurse at Wildfire.'

'I'm pleased to meet you, Hettie.' He hesitated and then went on. 'I'm very pleased to meet you. Without both of us... Well, we did the best we could.'

'You're injured. Those cuts need attention.'

'They do,' he agreed. 'I need disinfectant to avoid infection, but the alternative...'

'You never would have saved Joni without swimming over the coral,' she whispered, and once again she buried her face in the little boy's hair. 'Thank you.'

'I would have...I so wanted...'

'Yes,' she said gently. 'But she jumped too close to the rocks for either of us to do anything.'

'Depression?'

'Abuse. A bully for a husband. Despair.'

The bleakness in her voice must have been obvious. He reached out to her then, the merest hint of a touch, a trace of a strong hand brushing her cheek, and why it had the power to ground her, to feed her strength, she didn't know.

Max Lockhart was a big man, in his forties, she guessed, his deep black hair tinged with silver, his strongly boned face etched with life lines. His grey eyes were deep-set and creased at the edges, from weather, from sun, from...life? Even in his boxers, covered with abrasions, he looked... distinguished.

She knew about this man. He'd lost his wife over twenty years ago and he'd just lost his son. Caroline's twin.

'I'm sorry about Christopher,' she said gently, still holding Joni tight, as if holding him could protect him from the horrors around him.

'Caroline told you?'

'That her twin—your son—died three weeks ago? Yes. Caroline and I are fairly...close. She flew to Sydney for the funeral. We thought…we thought you might have come back with her.'

'There was too much to do. There was financial stuff to do with the island. To do with my brother. Business affairs have been on the backburner as Christopher neared the end, but once he was gone they had to be attended to. And then…'

'You thought it might be a good idea to sail out here?'

'I needed a break,' he said simply. 'Time to get myself together. No one warned me of cyclones.'

'It's the tropics,' she said simply. 'Here be dragons.'

'Don't I know it!'

'But we're glad you're back.'

That got her a hard look.

Max Lockhart had inherited the whole of Wildfire Island on the death of his father. The stories of the Lockharts were legion in this place. Max himself had hardly visited the island over the past twenty years, but his brother's presence had made up for it.

Ian Lockhart had bled the island for all it was worth. He'd finally fled three months ago, leaving debt, destruction and despair…

Ian Lockhart. The hatred he'd caused…

She hugged the child in her arms tighter, as if she could somehow keep protecting him.

How could she?

The sun was getting hotter. She was starting to get sunburnt. Sunburn on top of everything else?

She was wearing knickers and bra. But they were her best knickers and bra, though, she thought with sudden dumb gratitude that today of all days she'd decided to wear her matching lace bra and panties.

They were a lot more elegant than the boxers Max was wearing. His boxers were old, faded, and they now sported a rip that made them borderline useless.

'You needn't look,' Max said, and she flashed a look up at him and found he was smiling. And in return she managed a smile back.

Humour... It was a tool used the world over by medical staff, often in the most appalling circumstances. Where laypeople might collapse under strain, staff in emergency departments used humour to deflect despair.

Sometimes you laughed or you broke down, as simple as that, and right now she needed, quite desperately, not to break down. Max was a surgeon, she thought gratefully. Medical. Her tribe. He knew the drill.

'My knickers are more respectable than your knickers,' she said primly, and he choked.

'What? Your knickers are two inches of pink lace.'

'And they don't have a hole in them right where they shouldn't have a hole,' she threw back at him, and he glanced down at himself and swore. And did some fast adjusting.

'Dr Lockhart's rude,' she told Joni, snuggling him some more, but the little boy was drifting towards sleep. Good, she thought. Children had their own defences.

'My yacht seems to be escaping,' Max said, and she glanced back towards the reef.

It was, indeed, escaping. The anchor hadn't gripped the sand. The yacht was now caught in the rip and heading out to sea.

'One of the fishermen will follow it,' she told him. 'The rip's easy to read. They'll figure where it goes.'

'It'd be good to get to it now.'

'What could a yacht have that a good rock doesn't provide?' she demanded, feigning astonishment. And then she looked at his legs. 'Except maybe disinfectant and dressings. And sunburn cream.'

'And maybe a good strong rum,' he added.

'Trapped on an island with a sailor and a bottle of rum?

I don't think so.' She was waffling but strangely it helped. It was okay to be silly.

Silliness helped block the thought of what had to be faced. Of Sefina's body drifting out to sea…

'Tell me about yourself,' Max said, and she realised he was trying to block things out, too.

'What's to tell?' She shrugged. 'I'm Hettie. I'm charge nurse here. I'm thirty-five years old. I came to Wildfire eight years ago and I've been here ever since. I gather you've been here once or twice while I've been based here, but it must have coincided with my breaks off the island.'

'Where did you learn to swim?'

'Sydney. Bondi.'

'The way you swim… You trained as a lifesaver?'

'I joined as a Nipper, a trainee lifesaver, when I was six.' The surf scene at Bondi had been her tribe then. 'How did you know?'

'I saw how you took Joni from me,' he reminded her. 'All the right moves.'

'You were a Nipper, too?'

'We didn't have Nippers on Wildfire. I did have an aunt, though. Aunt Dotty. She knew the kids on the island spent their spare time doing crazier and crazier dives. I've dived off this headland more times than you've had hot dinners. We reckoned we knew the risks but Dotty said if I was going to take risks I'd be trained to take risks. So, like you, aged six I was out in the bay, learning the right way to save myself and to save others.' He shrugged. 'But until today I've never had to save anyone.'

'You are a surgeon, though,' she said gently, looking to deflect the bleakness. 'I imagine you save lots and lots.'

He smiled at that and she thought, *He has such a gentle smile.* For a big man…his smile lit his face. It made him seem younger.

'Lots and lots,' he agreed. 'If I count every appendix…'

'You should.'

'Then it's lots and lots and lots. How about you?'

'Can I count every time I put antiseptic cream on a coral graze?'

'Be my guest.'

'Then it's lots and lots and lots and lots and lots.'

And he grinned. 'You win.'

'Thank you,' she managed. 'It takes a big surgeon to admit we nurses have a place.'

'I've never differentiated. Doctors, nurses, even the ladies who do the flowers in the hospital wards and take a moment to talk… Just a moment can make a difference.'

And she closed her eyes.

'Yes, it can,' she whispered. 'I wish…oh, I wish…'

He'd stuffed it. Somehow they'd lightened the mood but suddenly it was right back with them. The greyness. The moment he'd said the words he'd seen the pain.

'What?'

Her eyes stayed closed. The little boy in her arms was deeply asleep now, cradled against her, secure for the moment against the horrors that had happened around him.

'What?' he said again, and she took a deep breath and opened her eyes again.

'I didn't have a moment,' she said simply. 'That'll stay with me for the rest of my life.'

'Meaning?'

'Meaning Sefina was brought into hospital just before the cyclone. Ruptured spleen. Concussion. Multiple abrasions and lacerations. Her husband had beaten her to unconsciousness. Sefina's not from M'Langi—she came here eighteen months ago from Fiji. Pregnant. Rumour is that… Joni's father…brought her here and paid Louis to marry her. Louis's an oaf. He'd do anything for money and he's treated her terribly. She's always been isolated and ashamed, and Louis keeps her that way.'

There was a moment's silence while he took that on board, and somehow during that moment he felt the beginnings of sick dismay. Surely it couldn't be justified, but once he'd thought of it he had to ask.

'So Joni's father...' he ventured, and she tilted her chin and met his gaze square on.

'He's not an islander.'

'Who?'

'Do I need to tell you?'

And he got it. He looked down at the little boy cradled in Hettie's arms. His skin wasn't as dark as the islanders'. His features...

His heart seemed to sag in his chest as certainty hit. 'My brother? Ian? He's his?' How had he made his voice work?

'Yes,' she said, because there was no answer to give other than the truth. 'Sefina is... Sefina *was* a Fijian islander. As far as I can gather, Ian stayed there for a while. He got her pregnant and she was kicked out of home. In what was a surprising bout of conscience for Ian, he brought her here. He paid Louis to marry her and he gave her a monthly allowance, which Louis promptly drank. But a few weeks ago the money stopped and Louis took his anger out on Sefina. The day before the cyclone things reached a crisis point. They were living out on Atangi. We flew her across to Wildfire, to hospital, but then the storm hit...and I didn't have that moment...'

'I'm sure you did your best.' It was a trite thing to say and he saw a flash of anger in response.

'She needed more.'

'She had no one else?'

'You need to understand. She was an outsider. She was pregnant by... And I'm sorry about this—but she was pregnant by a man the islanders have cause to hate. She married an oaf. Her mother-in-law wouldn't have anything to do with her, and vilified anyone who did. And the only person responsible—your brother—is now missing.'

'He's dead,' he said, and her gaze jerked to his.

'Dead?'

'That's another reason I couldn't get back here until now. Ian's been gambling—heavily. Unknown to me he racked up debts that'd make your eyes water. That's why he's bled the island dry. And that's why...well, his body was found two weeks ago, in Monaco. Who knows the whys or where-fores? The police are interested. I'm...not.'

There was a long, long silence.

She was restful, this woman, Max thought. Where others might have exclaimed, demanded details, expressed shock, disgust or horror, Hettie simply hugged the child in her arms a little tighter.

She was...beautiful, he thought suddenly.

Until now, despite the lacy knickers and bra, despite the attempt at humour, she'd seemed a colleague. A part of the trauma and the tragedy. Now, suddenly, she seemed more.

She was slight, five feet four or five. Her body was tanned and trim, and the lacy lingerie showed it off to perfection.

Her dark hair was still sodden. Her curls were forming wet spirals to frame her face.

Thirty-five, she'd said, and he might have guessed younger, apart from the life lines around her shadowed green eyes.

Life lines? Care lines? She'd cared about Sefina, he thought. She was caring about Joni.

Her body was curved around him now, protective, a lioness protective of her cub. Everything about her said, *You mess with this little one, you mess with me.*

His...nephew?

'You realise he's yours now,' she whispered at last into the stillness, and the words were like a knife, stabbing across the silence.

'What...?'

'This little boy is a Lockhart,' she said, deeply and evenly. 'The M'Langi islanders look after their own. Joni's not their own. He never has been. He was the child of two outsiders, and the fact that an oaf of an islander was paid to marry his mother doesn't make him belong. The islanders have one rule, which is inviolate. Family lines cross and intercross through the islands, but, no matter how distant, family is everything. Children can never be orphaned. The word "orphan" can't be translated into the M'Langi language.'

'What are you saying?' There was an abyss suddenly yawning before him, an abyss so huge he could hardly take it in.

She shrugged. 'It's simple,' she said softly. 'According to the M'Langi tradition, this little one isn't an orphan, Dr Lockhart. This little boy is yours.'

He had complications crowding in from all sides but suddenly they were nothing compared to this one.

Ian had had a son.

The boy didn't look like Ian, he thought. He had the beautiful skin colour of the Fijians but lighter. His dark hair wasn't as tightly curled.

He was still sleeping, his face nestled against Hettie's breast. Max could only see his profile, but suddenly...

It was a hint, a shade, a fleeting impression, but suddenly Max saw his mother in Joni.

And a hint of his own children. Caroline, twenty-six years old, due to be married next week to the man she loved.

Christopher, buried three weeks ago.

Christopher, his son.
This little boy is yours...

How could he begin to get his head around it? He couldn't. Every sense was recoiling.

He'd loathed Ian. Born of gentle parents, raised on this island with love and tenderness... There'd never been a reason why Ian should have turned out as he had, but he'd been the sort of kid who'd pulled wings off flies. He'd been expelled from three schools. He'd bummed around the world until his parents' money had dried up.

Max thought back to the time, a few years back, when Ian had come to see him in Sydney.

'I'm broke,' he'd said, honestly and humbly. 'I've spent the money Mum and Dad left me and I can't take the lifestyle I've been living anymore. I need to go back to Wildfire. Let me manage the place for you, bro. I swear I'll do a good job. We both know it's getting run-down and you don't have time to be there yourself.'

It was hope rather than trust that had made him agree, Max thought grimly. That and desperation. It had been true; the island had needed a manager. But Max had needed to be in Sydney. Christopher had been born with cerebral palsy and he'd lurched from one health crisis to another. Max had been trying to hold down a job as head of surgery at Sydney Central, feeding as much money as he could back into the island's medical services. Caroline, too... Well, his daughter had always received less attention than she'd needed or deserved.

If Ian could indeed take some of the responsibility...

Okay, he'd been naive, gullible, stupid to trust. That trust was coming home to roost now, and then some. He was having to face Ian's appalling dishonesty.

But facing this...
This little boy is yours...

His son was dead. How could he face this?

'You don't need to think about it now,' Hettie was saying gently, as if she guessed the body blow she'd dealt him. 'We'll work something out.'

'We?'

'I love Joni,' she said simply. 'I'm not going to hand him over until I'm sure you want him.'

'How can you love him?'

Her eyes suddenly turned troubled, even a little confused, as if she wasn't quite sure of what she was feeling herself. 'He has no one,' she said, tentatively now. 'His mother trusted me and depended on me. I was there at his birth.' She took a deep breath. 'Maybe...until you're ready to accept your responsibilities, I can take care of him for you.'

'My responsibility...'

'Whatever,' she said hastily. 'Until there's another alternative, I seem to be all he has. He needs someone. He has me.'

'You're not saying you'll take him on?'

'I'm not saying anything,' she whispered, and once again her lips touched the little one's hair. 'All I'm saying is that for now I'm holding him and I'm not letting go. Oh, and, Max...'

'Yes?'

'There are people on the beach,' she said. 'Waving. I think rescue is at hand. Time to get back to the real world.'

He glanced around sharply. There were, indeed, people on the beach.

'Caroline will be overjoyed,' Hettie told him. 'Your daughter. Your family.'

And there was something in the way she said it...

He knew nothing about her, he realised. Nothing at all. He was a Lockhart. The islanders, including Hettie, must know almost everything there was to know about him. But Hettie? He knew nothing about her other than she was holding...

His son?

CHAPTER THREE

THE CORAL CUTS on Max's legs were treated by his about-to-be son-in-law. Keanu, the island doctor Max's daughter was about to marry, greeted him with overwhelming relief, but was now insisting Max submit to his care.

It seemed Sam, the island's chief medical officer, had had to fly out that morning, transporting an urgent case to the mainland. 'We're always short on medical staff,' Keanu told him, 'so you're stuck with me. But I think we can get away with no stitches. Now, anaesthetic?'

'The last thing I need is a general anaesthetic,' Max growled. 'And no blocks. I've wasted enough of my time here. I don't intend to lie round, waiting for anaesthetic to wear off. Keanu, leave it. I can clean them myself.'

'So who'll explain to Caroline that you can't give her away because your legs are infected?' Keanu demanded. 'Not me. You'll let me clean them properly.'

So he had no choice. He lay back and thought about biting bullets as Keanu cleaned, disinfected and dressed his cuts.

Thankfully the cuts were on his legs and not his face, he thought. He might still manage to look okay at Caroline's wedding.

'You have no idea how relieved she'll be when she finds you're here,' Keanu told him as he worked. 'She's been out at a clinic at Atangi but she's due back any time now. Our wedding plans are all in order and now she has her dad. We were starting to think we'd have to send Bugsy down the aisle in your place.'

'Bugsy…'

'The dog,' Keanu said briefly, inspecting a graze that almost qualified as a cut. 'This one's nasty. Hold your breath for a bit, there's a bit of muck stuck in here.'

Max held his breath. Maybe an anaesthetic wouldn't have been such a bad idea.

'Dog,' he said at last when he could concentrate on anything other than pain.

'Bugsy, the golden retriever. He's responsible for us finding you so fast. Hettie left him on the beach. Normally Bugsy would loll around, waiting for her to come out of the water, or go for a swim himself, but he must have figured something was wrong. He came haring up to the hospital, soaking wet. We were already worried about Sefina and Joni. Sefina had discharged herself but we knew she couldn't go home, so when Bugsy appeared looking desperate, running back and forth to the beginning of the path to Sunset Beach, and we couldn't find Hettie, we put two and two together and figured we needed to investigate.'

'You let Sefina discharge herself?'

'Junior nurse,' Keanu said grimly. 'But it wasn't her fault. Short of holding Sefina by force, which was impossible, there wasn't a lot she could do when Sefina decided to leave. She let us know as soon as she could, and then Bugsy arrived.' He hesitated. 'Bugsy's a shared dog, devoted to all of us. He officially belongs to one of our fly in, fly out doctors, but Maddie's on maternity leave right now so Bugsy's main caregiver is Hettie.'

'Hettie has…no one else?'

Keanu cast him a sharp look. 'Hettie has everyone on the island.'

'Is that a warning?'

There was a moment's silence, and then Keanu gave a reluctant shrug. 'I know you're not Ian,' he conceded. 'I need to keep reminding the islanders.'

'Meaning they think if I was Ian I couldn't be trusted with anything in a skirt.'

'Ian couldn't be trusted with anything at all,' Keanu said bluntly. 'But he was your brother and Hettie tells me he's dead. I'm sorry.'

'Are you? Will anyone on this island be sorry?'

'No,' Keanu admitted bluntly. 'Maybe Sefina might have mourned him, but now...' He shrugged again, and then went back to focussing on Max's knee. 'Maybe a stitch here...'

'Steri-Strips,' Max growled. 'A scar or two won't hurt.'

'You can always cover it with pantyhose,' Keanu said, and grinned. 'It's good to have you home, Max. You've done so much for the island.' And then he glanced up as the door opened a crack. 'Hettie. Come in. That is, if Dr Lockhart doesn't mind you seeing his bare legs.'

'I saw a lot more than his legs out in the water,' Hettie retorted. 'And there's nothing our Dr Lockhart has that I haven't seen a thousand times before.'

'Shall we let the lady in?' Keanu asked.

And Max thought, *What the heck?* It was true, Hettie was a professional. Right now, he was a patient, she was a nurse. There was no reason he should feel odd at the idea of her seeing him dressed in a hospital gown with bare legs.

'Sure,' he growled, and Hettie popped in, smiling. It was a professional smile, he thought, just right, nurse greeting patient. She was in nurse's uniform, blue pants and baggy blue top. Her curls were caught back in a simple ponytail.

She looked younger than she'd looked on the atoll, he thought, and then he thought... She looked lovely?

She wasn't beautiful in the classical sense, he conceded.

Her nose was too snub, her cheeks were strong-boned, and her mouth was maybe too generous to be termed lovely.

She was wearing no make-up.

He still thought she looked beautiful.

'How's Joni?' Keanu asked, before Max could form the same question, and Hettie smiled, albeit sadly.

'Clean and dry and fast asleep in the kids' ward. He's the only occupant, now that any kids with minor injuries after the storm have gone home. I left Bugsy asleep beside his cot.'

'The dog?' Max stared. What sort of a hospital let dogs stay in the children's ward?

'We have monitors,' Hettie told him. 'The moment Joni stirs I'll be in there, but the first thing he'll see when he wakes will be Bugsy. Bugsy's a friend, and Joni...well, Joni needs all the friends he can get.'

'What will you do with him?' Keanu asked. Keanu was still cleaning. Hettie had moved automatically to assist, handing swabs, organising disinfectant. They were both focussed on Max's legs, which was disconcerting, to say the least.

The question hung and suddenly Max realised Keanu was talking to *him*.

What will you do with him?

'He's not mine to do anything with,' Max growled, and Keanu raised his brows.

'That's not what the islanders think.'

'They'll think he's yours,' Hettie said. 'I told you. He's your brother's child, your brother's dead, therefore he's your family. You don't want him?'

'Why would I want him?'

'Goodness knows,' Keanu said, and kept on working. It was disconcerting, to say the least, to be talking to two heads bent over his legs—plus talking about a child he'd only just learned existed. 'Family dynasty or something?' Keanu suggested. 'He is a Lockhart.'

'I have no proof he's a Lockhart.'

'You don't, do you?' Hettie was concentrating—fiercely, he thought—on his legs, and yet he could tell that her thoughts were elsewhere. On a little boy in the kids' ward. 'He could be anyone's.'

Yeah, but he looked like a Lockhart.

'Is there any sort of Child Welfare in the M'Langi group?' he asked.

'We don't need Child Welfare,' Hettie snapped, and Keanu cast her a surprised look. But then he shrugged and addressed Max.

'We don't normally need Child Welfare,' Keanu agreed. 'The islanders usually look after their own, but Joni's an exception. He's an outsider.'

'He's not an outsider. He belongs here, and if Max won't look after him, I will.' Hettie murmured the words almost to herself, but for a murmur it had power. The words were almost like a vow.

They made Keanu pause. The doctor stood back from the table and stared at Hettie, who was still looking at Max's legs fiercely.

'What the...? Het, are you suggesting you adopt him?'

'If no one else claims him, yes.'

'You can't decide that now.'

'I have decided. If his family doesn't want him, I do. I mean it. Keanu, do you want to keep cleaning or will I take over?'

Keanu stared at her for a moment longer and then silently went back to cleaning. There was a tense stillness, broken only by the sound of tiny chinks of coral hitting the kidney basin.

His legs really were a mess but, then, everything was a

mess, Max thought grimly. So what was new? When hadn't life been a mess?

For just a moment, this morning, watching the sun rise, watching the fish darting in and out of the water, watching a pod of dolphins give chase, he'd given himself time out. He'd thought, What if...?

What if he finally let himself be free?

Twenty-six years ago his wife had died on this island, giving birth to twins. He and Ellie had been babies themselves, barely twenty.

He'd met Ellie at university. They'd both been arts students, surrounded by friends, high on life. They'd fallen in love and when they'd discovered a baby was on the way they'd accepted the pregnancy with all the insouciance of youth.

'Maybe it's not a mistake,' Ellie had told him. 'Maybe we're meant to be a family.' The knowledge that she'd been carrying twins had only added to their feeling of excitement.

'How do you feel about marrying on Wildfire?' he'd asked, and she'd been ecstatic.

'The Lockhart family home? Your real-life island? Max, can we?'

They could, but not until summer vacation. They'd travelled to the island as soon as exams had ended. Ellie had been thirty-two weeks pregnant, excited about her pregnancy, excited about her sheer bulk.

He remembered their welcome. His mother had been wild with joy at their homecoming. His father had been gravely pleased that his son had found someone so beautiful to wed. No one had worried that Ellie had been pregnant at the ceremony. After all, what trouble could come to this truly blessed couple?

No one had worried that twin pregnancies sometimes spelled trouble.

He remembered his brother the night before the wedding. Ian had been blind drunk, toasting him for the hundredth time. They'd lit a campfire on the beach. Ian had waved his glass towards the island and then out at the stars hanging bright and low over the ocean.

'Here's to us, bro. We've got it all.'

He'd even been stupid enough to agree. The next day, he'd married. They'd danced into the small hours.

Ellie had gone into labour that night.

There had been no medical centre on the island then. They'd faced an agonising wait for medical evacuation, while Ellie had bled and bled.

She'd died before help arrived. The twins, Caroline and Christopher, had survived, but prematurity and birth trauma meant Christopher would be burdened with cerebral palsy for the rest of his life.

Christopher. His son.

'Family dynasty or something? He is a Lockhart.'

No. Christopher was his son, he thought grimly. Not some child called Joni. How could he ever want another child?

He closed his eyes and Keanu paused again.

'If this is hurting too much, let me knock you out.'

'Just go for it.'

There was silence as Keanu started work again. Undercurrents were everywhere, Max thought, gritting his teeth against the pain.

'Het, you won't be able to just...adopt him,' Keanu said at last into the stillness. 'You'll have to go through channels. If it's really what you want then we'll support you, but you're not deciding this today. This suggestion seems right out of the blue. It's a huge decision and there are legal channels to be dealt with. You know we come under Australian legal jurisdiction. If Joni doesn't have relatives on the island...' Here he cast a quick glance at Max. 'As the island's acting medical director, I'll need to report Sefina's death and Joni's status to the mainland authorities. A kid like Joni…there'd be mainland couples lined up to adopt a toddler like him. You'll need to plead some special case to be allowed to keep him.'

'Sefina was my friend,' Hettie told him.

'Sefina was your patient.'

'I let her down.'

'We all let her down but her death is not our fault. I'm not about to let a guilty conscience force you into adoption.'

'I'm not being forced.'

'Why would you want to adopt?' Max asked, and they both paused in their work, as if they'd forgotten he was there.

Maybe they should have had this discussion without him, Max thought. After all, it had nothing to do with him. Just because it was Ian's child…

This little boy is yours.

No. He wanted nothing to do with Ian's child.

His own son was dead. His daughter was about to be married to the man of her dreams and he might even be free of another responsibility.

All his life he'd accepted the responsibility the Lockharts had carved for themselves through generations of ownership. Every spare cent he'd earned had been ploughed back into this hospital. He'd worked so hard…

But now… In the next couple of days Max would meet the man who'd funded a world's best tropical diseases research facility and tropical resort on Wildfire. Ian had conned a Middle Eastern oil billionaire—a sheikh, no less—into purchasing island land for the resort, but the sale had been built on forged signatures and falsehoods. Island land was held in a Lockhart family trust for perpetuity and Ian had had no power to sell. Amazingly, though, once he'd known the facts, the sheikh had still been prepared to invest, leasing instead of buying. He had seemingly limitless money and resources. He was giving work to the islanders, giving hope, and for the first time since that night before his wedding, twenty-six years ago, Max was feeling a taste of freedom.

Maybe he could walk away from here and never come back.

This little boy is yours. Hettie's words, Keanu's words meant nothing. They couldn't. He did not want any more responsibility.

But finally Hettie was answering his question. 'I want to adopt because I can,' she said. It was as if she'd needed time to work out her answer, but now she had it clear. 'I've spent my life looking out for no one but myself. Sitting out on the atoll this morning, holding Joni, knowing Sefina was dead, it crowded in on me. I give nothing. I love…nothing. If I can have Joni…I will love him, Keanu. I promise.'

'But it won't be up to me,' Keanu told her, giving her a searching look. 'We'll report Sefina's death to the authorities and see what happens.'

'I won't let him leave the island.'

'Het, the islanders won't accept him,' Keanu said gently. 'He's Ian's child and Ian robbed them blind.'

'He'll be my child.'

'Let's see what the authorities say.' Keanu fastened a last dressing on Max's legs. 'There you go, Dr Lockhart. All better. You're free to go.'

Free to go…

It sounded okay to him, Max thought, swinging his legs gingerly from the examination table. Hettie held his arm while he stood, and he had the sense to let her. Lying supine during medical procedures could make anyone dizzy.

And dizziness did come, just a little, but it was enough for him to be grateful for Hettie's support.

She was small and slight. She'd been through an appalling experience, too, and yet he could feel her strength. She was some woman. How many women would have backed up such a morning with heading into work; with continuing to keep going?

With offering to adopt a child?

'Are you okay?' Hettie asked, sounding worried.

She was worried about him?

'I'm fine. Just a bit wobbly.'

'Take your time,' Keanu told him. 'We'll find you a bed in the ward.'

'If you can find me some clothes I'll head up to the house.' His clothes were either in the water or on board the boat. And where was his boat?

'You need someone to keep an eye on you,' Hettie said. 'With those legs, you need care. I'm not sure where Caroline is…'

And, as if on cue, the doors to the theatre swung open. Caroline burst through the doors, looking frantic.

'Dad,' she said as she saw him. 'Oh, Dad…' And she flung herself into his arms and burst into tears.

Hettie stepped back.

'You'll be okay now,' she said softly. 'You're with your family.'

And she walked out and left him with his daughter.

Keanu was waiting as Hettie finished her interview with the local constabulary. He'd protested as she'd donned her nurse's uniform instead of civvies the moment she'd reached the hospital. Now, though, with Max settled with his daughter and Joni asleep, there seemed no reason for her to stay. The hospital on Wildfire had settled to a new norm. Without Sefina.

Hettie could hardly think of Sefina without wanting to be sick. Of all the senseless deaths…

'There's nothing more you can do, Het,' Keanu told her as the policeman left. The young doctor was starting to sound stern. 'You've had an appalling shock. For you and Max to save Joni was little short of miraculous. You need to give your body time to recover. Take Bugsy home with you and sleep.'

'How can I sleep? Keanu, we failed her.'

'The island failed her,' he said. 'The islanders hated Ian Lockhart, and Sefina was someone they could vent that anger on.'

'It wasn't her fault.'

'We all know that. Even the islanders know that. It was only her husband who was overtly cruel and he'll be prosecuted. Now you need to take care of you.'

'I'll stay with Joni.'

'Not on my watch, Het,' he said, even more firmly. 'Joni's a problem we need to solve but not now, not when you're emotionally distraught. If I let you stay with him all the time it'll tear your heart out when he leaves. I don't know where your offer of adoption came from, but it's crazy. You know it is. You haven't had time yet even to absorb the enormity of Sefina's death. So let's be professional. We're taking care of him. Go home.'

'I don't want to.'

'I'll give you something to help you sleep,' he said, as if he hadn't heard her objection, and he took her shoulders and propelled her to the nurses' station. 'But you're signing off now and that's an order.'

It was all very well, following orders, but Hettie needed to work. She was exhausted but work seemed the only way to get the events of the morning out of her head.

She couldn't—but neither could she get rid of this certainty of what she had to do.

She'd tried hard not to get emotionally involved with her patients. Why did she suddenly, fiercely, want to adopt Joni?

Why did she *need* to adopt Joni?

She walked slowly around the lagoon, in no hurry to get to her neat little villa overlooking the water. The island was lush, beautiful, washed with rain. Most of the storm damage had been cleared. A few palms had fallen but tropical rain forest regenerated fast. Soon there'd be nary a scar.

Except Sefina was dead.

Maybe it'd be easier, she thought, if there was a body to bury. To keen over?

It'd be a tiny funeral if the body was ever found. Nobody here had loved Sefina.

No one would love Joni. He was Ian Lockhart's son.

He'd be adopted off the island, she thought bleakly. Here he'd never get over the stigma of being Ian's son. He'd never be accepted.

'I could make him be accepted.' She said it out loud but even as she said it she faced its impossibility. On this island Joni was an illegitimate outsider. He always would be.

'But I want him.'

Why? She sank onto a fallen log and stared sightlessly over the lagoon. Why did she want, so fiercely, to hug Joni to her? To hold?

Her maternal instinct was long dead. Killed by Darryn...

'Oh, get over it.' She rose and stared out at a heron standing one legged at the edge of the water. She often saw this guy here. He was a lone bird.

'And that's what I am, too,' she told herself. 'Today was an aberration. Joni will find himself some lovely parents on the mainland who'll love him to bits. And I...' She took a deep breath. 'I'll take the pills Keanu gave me and go to sleep. And I'll wake up in the morning feeling not maternal at all. I'll feel back to normal.'

But she couldn't stop thinking of Joni.

And, strangely, she couldn't stop thinking of Max. Max, swimming strongly towards her in the water as she felt herself pulled out to sea. Max, risking his life to save a woman he didn't know, almost killing himself in the process. Max, tugging a small child from a dead woman's arms.

A decent Lockhart?

She'd watched his face when he'd told her Sefina was dead. She knew it had almost killed him to release her body, to make the choice to save her son instead.

He'd be feeling sick, too. She knew it.

Would Max stay in hospital for the night? Would Keanu insist he stay, or would he let Caroline take him home to the big house, the homestead owned by the Lockharts for generations?

'So what's that got to do with you?' she demanded of herself. 'You've never had anything to do with the Lockharts.'

Which wasn't quite true. As nurse administrator she'd had conflict after conflict with Ian Lockhart. The funds for the medical administration came from the Australian government, augmented by donations from a trust Max Lockhart had set up when his wife had died. Ian, however, had swaggered onto the island a few years back and had tried to take control. For a while, because of his name, they'd let him sit on the hospital board but pretty soon they'd realised the hospital hadn't been a priority. Equipment had been purchased from the trust but had mysteriously never appeared. If she hadn't been on the ball…

She had been. There'd been an almighty row, she'd threatened to bring in lawyers and she and Ian had hardly spoken after that.

Max looked like his brother.

They were so different…Ian was a con man, out for what he could get, morally empty.

This morning Max Lockhart had risked his life trying to save a woman and her child.

Max had poured money into this island's medical services for years.

Max had mourned his dead wife and had cared for his son until the end.

'Yeah, he's a hero, and he looks great in boxers.' She ran her hand through her hair and her tight ponytail came free, letting her curls cascade to her shoulders. She hauled them back up with something akin to anger.

She was so confused.

No, she thought. What she was feeling was shock. It'd be shock making her thoughts so tumultuous.

'So go home and sleep,' she said out loud. 'You know that's the most sensible thing to do. Go home and stop thinking of Joni. And stop thinking of Max.'

She tried. The pills Keanu had given her put her to sleep but her sleep was full of dreams.

Sefina's body, drifting on the tide.

A little boy, unloved, lying alone in the hospital ward.

Max Lockhart.

Why was he superimposing himself over all the rest?

Despite Keanu's objections, Max discharged himself. 'I have my own home and my daughter's a qualified nurse. She can report in if my condition gets interesting,' he'd told Keanu. So Caroline drove him the short distance to the Lockhart homestead, but once in the jeep a silence fell between Max and his daughter.

Where to start? There'd been silence between them for twenty-six years, he thought grimly. He hadn't treated her fairly and he knew it. He'd had two children. Ninety five per cent of his attention had been taken by Christopher. Caroline had had to fit into the edges.

'Caro,' he started, dubiously, and she flashed him a look that might even have been amusement.

'You're going to say sorry again?'

'There's not a lot else to say. I shouldn't have tried sailing here. Hettie says you were terrified.'

'I was.'

'And…I shouldn't have left you alone for so long.' He had to say it. He'd had no choice, but now that Christopher was dead the ghosts had to be hauled into the open. 'I'm so pleased you and Keanu are together.' Keanu was an island kid, grown up to be a fine doctor. He was loyal, intelligent and courageous. There was no one he'd rather have for a son-in-law, but that Caroline had met him and was marrying him was in no way down to her father. He'd done so little for her.

'Dad, I understand.' They pulled up in front of the homestead. She switched off the ignition but made no move to get out. 'Yes, there were times during my childhood when I resented the time you spent with Christopher, but the older I get the more I understand. You could never have looked after two babies on your own, not with Christopher's needs. And Grandma and Aunt Dotty were wonderful. I had Keanu as a playmate and his mum as our housekeeper. I had this whole island and I had freedom. If you'd taken me to Sydney I'd have had childcare and no one apart from the snatches of time you could spare.'

'I should have spared more.'

'And taken that time from Christopher? How could you?' She put her hand on his and held. 'Dad, you know I loved him. You know how much I wanted him to live— how much I've been hoping a miracle would save him. That last rally, I so hoped… It wasn't to be, but my comfort was that you were there, loving him for me, for us, right to the end. I guess I've accepted now that he was always on borrowed time, but it must have broken your heart, watching him fade. Yet all the while you've supported the medical needs of this island every way you know how. And I know you're blaming yourself for Ian's dishonesty but maybe you had to trust him. Ian was *your* brother, and this was his island, too.'

Redemption? Forgiveness? His daughter was handing it to him, but could he take it? His legs ached. His head hurt. The morning's tragedy hung heavily in his thoughts.

So much tragedy…

'Hey!' Caroline released her seat belt and gave him a hug and then kissed him. 'Don't look like that. Dad, it's over. The new guy investing in the resort is pouring money into the island—did you know he wants to help with the medical facilities, as well? I know there are legal things you have to sort, but they're minor. And, Dad…Christopher's dead. You did everything you could do for him, but now it's over. And I'm marrying the man of my dreams. For the first time in your life you're responsible for nobody, for nothing. You're free, Dad. It's time you shook off the guilt and enjoyed yourself.'

'And Joni?' He said it heavily, as if he couldn't help himself, and maybe he couldn't. 'Joni's a Lockhart. I can't escape that.'

Caroline took a deep breath. 'So he is,' she said gently. 'So I guess he's my cousin. If no one else will take him, maybe Keanu and I could.'

'You can't go into a marriage with someone else's child.'

'Honestly, it's not something I ever planned for,' she said diffidently. 'But if Joni is indeed my cousin… Dad, we may have no choice.'

'That's crazy. The social welfare system works well for orphaned children. Lots of families will want him.'

'Dad, you don't understand.' Caroline put her hand on

his. 'You were born here. You should get it. According to the islanders, Joni's now yours.'

'How can he be mine?' He felt as if a vast leaden weight was descending onto his shoulders. 'Hettie wants him,' he said abruptly, and Caroline's eyes widened.

'Hettie?'

'She wants to adopt him.'

'That's crazy.' She shook her head in disbelief. 'She's shocked. It's been an appalling morning. She'll be devastated by Sefina's death. We're all upset but as for taking him on...'

'Yet you're saying you could take him.'

'It wouldn't work with Hettie,' Caroline said, thinking it through. 'He'd be the illegitimate son of an outsider, with the stigma of Ian as a father to add to it. He'd have no father to watch his back. If Keanu and I adopted him, the islanders would know he's our family. They love Keanu. They'd come to accept him soon enough.'

'But he's my responsibility.' There. He'd said it. The words were heavy and hard, but they were true. Whether he liked it or not, he was the closest kin. To have a situation where his daughter took on that responsibility because he wouldn't...

It made him feel ill, but what was the alternative?

Adoption off the island? It *was* an option, but no one else was seeing it.

'You're tired,' Caroline said at last into the stillness. 'Come into the house. You can have some sandwiches and those nice painkillers Keanu's given you. Then you can sleep until morning. Problems always seem smaller in the morning.'

'I need to visit the mine. I need to talk to—'

'You need to do nothing except sleep,' she said soundly. 'Bed, this instant.'

'Yes, Mum,' he said meekly, and she chuckled and

hugged him, and he thought that at least he was here with his daughter.

But...why was he still thinking of Hettie?

CHAPTER FOUR

SLEEP WAS NOWHERE. At 3:00 a.m. Hettie lay staring into the dark, and ghosts she'd thought were long buried resurfaced and started swirling.

Dawn, long ago, a morning like this one. Breakers hurling in from the east, pounding the beach. The lingering remnants of a vast southerly storm.

Darryn, waking her, exuberant with excitement. He'd organised the press for a photo shoot.

'Come on, babe. The surf's perfect.'

She'd protested, still sleepy, still tired. 'Darryn, the waves are huge. You know the doctor said—'

'Honey, the doctor's just covering himself. Our kid's born to surf. Honest, he'll come out hanging ten. Let's go.'

'I don't want to.' There, she'd said it. 'I'm seven months pregnant. I'm off balance on my board. It's dangerous.'

'You're not turning into a wuss on me. Babe, I married you because you're a surfing legend. The pictures will be awesome. Come on!'

And now, sixteen years on, her hands moved instinctively to her belly.

For sixteen years she'd buried this hunger. Today one little boy had unleashed it to the extent it was threatening to overwhelm her.

She couldn't go back to sleep. She was trying to be logical but logic was nowhere. All she could see when she closed her eyes was Max, in the water, holding his arms out for Joni. Demanding she release him to keep him safe.

She could still feel the wrench as she'd let him go. A little boy who needed her.

How could she let him go again?

This was nonsense. It was emotional fluff. She had no business to be thinking of it.

But she was more than thinking of it. She was tossing back the bedclothes, tugging on jeans and heading for the children's ward.

He was in the bedroom he'd moved into when he'd married.

When he'd been a kid Max had had a small room at the back of the house. From his window he'd been able to see all the way to the sea.

But Caroline had that bedroom now. She'd assumed he'd want to sleep in this big room. This place of ghosts.

He and Ellie had hardly had any time at all here, he thought bleakly. A break from university while they'd planned the wedding, the wedding itself, and then tragedy.

Ellie had given birth in this bed. How could a man sleep in it?

It was history. Twenty-six years of history.

He'd decided to come back now, see Caroline married, sort out the financial affairs with the sheikh who was prepared to pour money into the place and then walk away.

For the first time since the birth of the twins he'd be responsible for nobody.

Except one little boy. Fifteen months old.

A Lockhart.

Caroline had suggested she could take him on. She would, too, he thought. His daughter had a heart big enough to take on all comers. But, like him, she had her whole future ahead of her. She was marrying Keanu.

He couldn't—he wouldn't—ask them to take on Joni.

Hettie, then?

A single woman. A woman who'd instinctively said she'd care.

It'd be different in the morning, he thought. Hettie would be back to being sensible.

So… Adoption off the island…

Why did that feel so wrong?

This little boy is yours.

'I'm too much of an islander,' he said into the dark. 'But I don't believe it. The child needs parents who want him. Adoption's the only way.'

This little boy is yours.

And suddenly he was thinking of a toddler, waking in the small hours, calling from his cot. As Christopher had called for him.

Where was sleep when he needed it? Nowhere?

He lay and stared into the dark until the dark seemed to take shapes and mock him.

This little boy is yours.

Useless. He swore and threw back the sheets. He hauled on pants and a shirt and headed for the children's ward.

The children's ward was empty, apart from Joni. 'He's asleep,' the night nurse told Hettie. 'I checked on him twenty minutes ago.'

But he wasn't asleep anymore. He was lying on his back, wide-eyed, staring upward. The ward had luminescent stars all over the ceiling but Hettie wouldn't mind betting Joni wasn't looking at the stars. He seemed almost to be looking past them. He had a corner of the sheet in his mouth and was sucking fiercely, but he wasn't making a sound.

'Louis hits us both if Joni cries,' Sefina had told her. 'Joni's good, but he can't be good forever.'

'Joni?' she said softly, and the baby's gaze flicked to her and then away again. He went on sucking fiercely.

'Hey.' It was too much. Hettie scooped him up and cradled him against her. He was stiff and unresponsive. She tugged the sheet with her so he could keep on sucking. Anything that gave him comfort was okay by her. Anything...

'How is he?'

It was a low growl. Max. He was standing in the doorway. She wasn't startled. For some reason it seemed almost inevitable that he was here.

'He should be crying,' Hettie whispered. 'But even so young he's been trained not to cry. With his stepfather... there were consequences.'

'You're kidding.' Max spoke softly, his words seeming little more than another shadow in the night. 'What kind of creep...?'

'He's nothing to do with Joni anymore.' Hettie kissed Joni on the top of his head. 'Louis didn't let Sefina name him as father on the birth certificate. She named Ian. He never adopted Joni so he has no hold. No one will hurt you, little one. You're safe with me.'

She stood and rocked while Max watched. He could retreat. There was no need for him to stay.

He stayed.

'He's not sleepy?'

'Are any of us?' Hettie asked hollowly, and Max shrugged.

'Not me.' Then he looked up at the ceiling. 'How about bringing him outside so we can see some real stars?'

She nodded without a word, and carried the little boy out through the glass doors to the courtyard and down to the lagoon beyond. The courtyard and walkway down to the lagoon were set up so healing patients could lie under the palms, still under the watchful eye of the staff on duty. Hettie sank down onto one of the loungers, still cradling Joni.

Most children would be wailing, Max thought. It was the middle of the night. Joni was with strangers. Why wasn't he sobbing for his mother?

How did you train a child not to cry? The question made him feel cold.

'See the stars?' Hettie whispered to Joni. 'See how many there are? They're up there, guarding us. Every one of them is your friend. Aren't they, Max?'

'They surely are.'

'And the moon's the biggest friend of all. He watches over the whole sky and keeps us safe.'

She almost had him believing it.

He sat on the lounger beside them while Hettie crooned her words of comfort to the little boy. In truth, he wasn't quite sure what he was doing here. Keeping guard? That's what it felt like, but who needed guards when there was Old Man Moon and his minion stars?

But it felt okay. More, it almost felt as if something inside him was settling. The last few weeks had been fraught and this day had been steeped in tragedy and grief. Sitting here under the stars with this gentle woman brought a measure of peace.

Around them was strewn the detritus from the cyclone. Trees had been uprooted, stripped foliage was everywhere and clearing up had barely started, yet here the darkness hid the damage. Here was an oasis of calm. Here was peace.

Hettie rocked and rocked, and then she started a gentle singing, a silly little tune that children must know the world over.

'My nanny sang that to me,' Max said softly, as he watched Joni's body finally lose its rigidity. The little boy was slumped, exhausted, against Hettie's breast, as if he'd finally lost the fight. He had no one else to turn to. Hettie was his last resort and he may as well submit.

'My grandma sang it to me, too,' Hettie whispered back between tunes. 'Hush, little one. Sleep.'

And amazingly Joni did. His eyes fluttered as he fought against the inevitable but finally he slept.

There was a long silence, broken only by the faint lapping of the water at the edges of the lagoon. It felt okay, Max thought. It felt good.

'Did you sing it to your twins?' Hettie asked at last.

'To Christopher,' he said shortly. 'I had to leave Caroline behind.'

'On the island?'

'Yes.'

He didn't tell people his personal business, but suddenly it was out there. A long-ago tragedy.

'My wife went into labour here on the island,' he said. 'We had no medical facilities. The twins were premature and came fast. Caroline was four pounds, big enough to survive. Christopher was only three. He survived but with cerebral palsy. Ellie haemorrhaged and died the day before she could be evacuated.'

'I guess... I knew that much,' she said. 'That's why you set up the hospital.'

'I was twenty.' He said it with muted fury, remembering the waste, the realisation of a loss he could never make good. 'We were arts students, studying in Sydney, young enough to think we knew everything. We came home to the island in our summer vacation to shock everyone with our pregnancy and to marry. We never thought...'

'Kids don't.' She hugged Joni a little tighter.

'So I grew up fast,' he said. 'Christopher needed excellent medical care. I decided there and then that Wildfire was going to get the best medical facilities I could manage, but I couldn't care for twins, not with Christopher's needs. So Caroline stayed here with my mother—her grandma. She came to Sydney later when she was ready for boarding school. I went back straight away, though. I moved from studying arts to medicine. I studied and I cared for Chris. Then I worked and cared for Chris. So, yes, I sang to Chris but I never sang to Caro.'

'She doesn't resent it,' Hettie said softly, as if she guessed his bone-deep grief. 'I'm sure she understands.'

'It doesn't stop me feeling like I've failed her,' he said heavily. 'At least she has Keanu now. At least she has someone who she knows will love her.'

'I'm sure she knows you love her.'

He paused and stared at Joni and tried to get his thoughts in order. 'We should never have got pregnant,' he said at last. 'We were two kids without a sense of responsibility between us. It was an accident but we weren't being careful. Planning a baby is huge.'

'It is.'

'And yet you say you want Joni.'

'Yes.'

'Within a day of his mother dying. It's an impulse decision.'

'That doesn't make it bad. Having Christopher and Caroline…no, it wasn't planned but they were loved. Joni will be loved.'

More silence. Sitting under the stars with this woman seemed to lead to silence. There was something about her, he thought, some restful quality that seemed to make his world settle. The huge bundle of regret and grief that had been his world since Christopher's death all at once seemed to take a step back.

'Tell me about you,' he said into the night, and was it his imagination or did she stiffen?

'What about me?'

'You know about me,' he told her. 'Max Lockhart, owner of Wildfire Island, brother of criminal Ian, father of Caroline…'

'Uncle of Joni,' she added, and he winced.

'Don't. Just tell me about you. You're the head nurse here. You've been here for years. Did you come here to escape?'

'Why would I do that?'

'People do. My great-great-grandfather bought this place as an escape after a scandal with a married woman. He brought her here, waited for years for her divorce to come through and then married her with all honour. But the initial decision to buy the island was as an escape.'

'I didn't know that.'

'You have no idea how many skeletons there are in the Lockhart family closet. So show me one of yours. Why did you run here?'

'I didn't!'

And for a while he thought she wouldn't say more. It didn't actually matter if she didn't, he decided. The night was warm and still, Joni was deeply asleep and the sky was aglow with stars. There was a sense of peace that couldn't be messed with, no matter what skeletons were exposed.

'I'll tell you,' she said at last, though. 'If you'll support me caring for Joni.'

'I can't decide if you can have Joni.'

'No. Sorry. I guess… All I'm thinking is that you're Joni's uncle. You deserve to know a little about the woman who's fighting for custody, and I will need your support.'

'So you will fight for custody?'

'Yes.' She said it harshly, and Joni stirred uneasily in her arms. She hushed and crooned and Joni slipped back to sleep, and Max sat on while she decided what she wanted to tell him.

'I was a bit like you,' she said at last. 'I married young. My parents were surfers, hippies, based at Bondi Beach in Sydney but following the waves. I learned to surf when I was three but they often left me behind. My grandma was my rock. She died when I was fifteen and after that I sort of drifted. But by then, wow, I could surf. I was competitive. I won a couple of world championships and then I met Darryn.'

'Your husband.'

'We thought we were so cool,' she told him. 'Both champion surfers. Both invincible. We had this crazy, amazing wedding on the beach in Hawaii. We had the world at our feet—nothing could touch us.' She shrugged. 'Only then I fell pregnant and I was fat and clumsy and I backed off in the surf. Darryn wasn't doing too well, either, and he couldn't stand it. He hated not being in the limelight. Finally he organised a photo shoot with one of the big American surfing magazines. He said it'd be stunning publicity, me hanging ten when I was so pregnant. It'd tell the world why we weren't out front in the surf scene anymore. But on the day, the swell was huge. I should never have agreed to do it.'

'And…' He hated to ask but he had to.

She sighed. 'And something went horribly wrong. To this day I have no idea how, but I bombed and the board hit my belly. I lost my baby and I also lost the chance to have any more children.'

'Oh, Hettie…'

'So Darryn couldn't cope with my grief,' she said, as if she hadn't heard him interrupt. 'He left me as soon as he decently could. I went back to Sydney, knowing I had to make a living. I scraped through a nursing course but I hated being anywhere I could meet any old friends. I got the best qualifications I could, and then this job came up. I've been here ever since.'

'So you're hiding?'

'I'm not hiding,' she snapped, and then bit her lip as Joni stirred again. 'This is my family. I love the island, the islanders, the hospital, my colleagues. I'd never had a place to call home until I reached here. This is where I want to be.'

'And now you want a baby?'

'I didn't know I did,' she murmured, cradling Joni to her. 'I thought I'd blocked it out. Until today. Until I held him. Suddenly I realised that this was someone I could help. He's injured, Max. Not just today, though heaven knows how he'll remember the terror of today. But he's already had his tiny lifetime marred by abuse at the hands of the man who was supposed to be his father. He's been hit. Sefina told me on that last appalling day when she was admitted. He's seen his mother being hit. How old do you have to be to remember such things? All I know is that he's quiet when he should cry. I know his background. I knew Sefina, and I can bring him up to love her. I've been thinking and thinking. It may seem selfish to you, but it's not. I can give him…all the love he needs and more. If he's adopted on the mainland this part of his life will be a blank. It shouldn't be. He needs to be here.'

'And you need him.' It wasn't a question.

'Maybe I do,' she said softly. 'Maybe until today I didn't realise how much. But I will look after him. We will be a family.'

'He might not be accepted on the island.'

'Because he's Ian's? He's not Ian's. He's mine.'

Was there anything else to be said? There were questions everywhere, Max thought, but he couldn't voice them.

He should go back to bed. His legs ached and he had a power of issues to face in the morning. Ian had left a legacy of debt and deceit. He needed to start sorting the mess. The sooner he got it sorted, the sooner he could leave.

But somehow, tonight, the thought of leaving was slipping into soft focus. Ever since Ellie had died, twenty-six years ago, he'd thought he hated this island. The horror of Sefina's suicide should have made it worse.

Somehow it didn't, though. Somehow, sitting here in the

peace of the night, with this woman, with this child, the grief of the past seemed to lessen.

'Has Caroline told you all her wedding plans?' Hettie asked.

And he thought, *Great, we're moving on, away from the grey of the past*. But there was another shadow.

'I guess she doesn't have to. She'll have it all arranged.'

'She hasn't run things by you?'

'She's been independent forever. She's known she can't count on her dad.'

'She's known why,' Hettie said gently. 'You can't beat yourself up over something that's not your fault.'

'You'd be amazed at what I can beat myself up over.'

'Well, that makes two of us.' She grinned. 'Glum and Glummer, that's us. It doesn't help, though. Tell you what, how about a swim tomorrow?'

'The sea...' he said, startled, and she shook her head.

'Not in the surf. I'm no longer a surfer. You needn't worry, a wave doesn't have to be very big to have me a screaming wuss and backing away.'

'You weren't a wuss today.'

'Neither were you. No choice gives us no choice. But below the resort...'

'The resort?'

'The research station. You know it? Have you seen it yet? I don't suppose you have. But you must know that Sheikh al Taraq—or Harry, as he's known, the guy who's rebuilt the research centre—has converted it into a world-class conference venue. It'll take your breath away. I know you're leasing the land to him. I know the scandal. Every-one here knows now that Ian conned him into thinking the land was his, but he seems to have accepted the facts and moved on. So as owner I reckon you need to do a tenancy inspection, and if you do, how about in your swimming gear? There's a lagoon between the resort and the sea. It's fed by rainwater from the mountains so it won't hurt your legs—but you'll know that.'

Then she glanced at Max's legs and grimaced. 'Okay, maybe not tomorrow,' she conceded. 'Maybe tomorrow's for sitting on the verandah and trying not to wince. But by Tuesday you should be up for a swim. It might even do you good. I swim most mornings so if you're up for it…Tuesday morning? Seven o'clock?'

'Hettie…'

'I know, you have a power of stuff to face,' she said, gently again. 'And so do I. Neither of us may be able to do it. But if we can… Look, it's just a thought. I'll be at the track at the back of the house at seven. If you're there, you're there. If you're not, you're not, and no hard feelings.' And then she stood, still cradling Joni. 'That's it,' she said briskly. 'Time to move on. Goodnight, Dr Lockhart.'

'Goodnight, Hettie.'

She smiled and gave a brisk little nod and turned away.

He stood and watched her as she walked back into the hospital. A woman holding his nephew. A woman claiming him as her own?

The child was a Lockhart, if not in name, certainly in everything else.

Hettie wanted Joni.

And Max… Who knew what he wanted?

Hettie disappeared and he dug his hands into his pockets and gazed back out over the lagoon.

He could settle things here and disappear, to a life, finally with no responsibilities.

That's what he'd thought he wanted. So why did watching a woman disappear into the darkened hospital suddenly make him feel…hungry?

Hettie returned Joni to his cot, then settled in a chair beside him. There was no need to stay—the night staff would be here in moments if there was a peep out of him—but somehow it seemed impossible to leave him. Whatever ties had been created in the morning's drama seemed to be strengthening by the moment. She couldn't leave him.

She might have to. She had no right to him. He was an orphan. Keanu had already told her that the mainland social services had been contacted. She'd have to fight.

'And I will,' she whispered into the night, and part of that fight seemed to start right now. She fetched a rug from the linen bank, tugged it over herself and tried to settle.

But not to sleep. Sleep was nowhere. The events of the day were too horrific.

Joni's needs were too overwhelming.

Max's presence was too…invasive.

What was that about?

She didn't know. All she did know was that every time she closed her eyes, instead of the horrors of the day, somehow superimposed was Max.

Max, sitting beside the lagoon, gazing reflectively into the night. Max, describing his past, the pain of choices he'd had no part in making.

Max, taking Joni from her just as she'd felt herself sweeping out to sea, out of control. Saving her baby.

Not her baby. Joni.

Max, trying with everything he had to save Sefina.

She shouldn't be thinking of Max. The day had been a swirl of trauma. There was so much else to be thinking of besides Max, so why did he seem beside her now? Why had sitting beside him on the edge of the lagoon seemed to settle not just the terrors of today but past terrors?

She'd asked him to go swimming with her. How stupid was that?

He wouldn't come. Even if his legs didn't hurt, why would he come?

But if he did…

Stop thinking about it, she told herself fiercely. Her life was suddenly complicated. It'd get more complicated if she was to have a hope of adopting Joni, and stupid teenage thoughts about a guy with a good body could mess things completely.

But he has more than a good body. She almost said it aloud but she was in the hospital so the monitors were on and anything she said could be heard at the nurses' station. She still had some remnants of sense.

Did she want...more than a good body?

The question was suddenly out there. Why?

Relationships terrified her. She'd stepped into marriage that one horrendous time and the scars were still with her. She'd made a vow to stay single, to stay in control, for the rest of her life.

So why was Max Lockhart messing with that control? Why did the image of him, the sound of his voice, make something inside her feel as if it was stretching to breaking point?

'It was the day,' she said, and it seemed her subconscious was taking over her sense as well as her thoughts because she did say it out loud. 'It's just the way he held Joni and the way he saved him—it's the way he saved me... We both could have drowned without him. It's made me feel vulnerable.'

But...vulnerable? Was that the word she was looking for?

She was gazing down at the sleeping Joni, aching to lift him and hold him again. But there was suddenly a deeper ache, and it was an ache she couldn't acknowledge. She couldn't begin to define it. Max...

But she had spoken out loud, and Beth, the nurse on duty, was bustling down the corridor to see what was happening.

'Hettie? Is anything wrong?'

'No.' It was as much as Hettie could do not to snap but

somehow she managed it. She was off balance and if she was to have a chance to adopt Joni then she needed to be more on balance than she'd ever been in her life. She certainly didn't need to be letting her subconscious have weird thoughts about his uncle. 'I'm just muttering to myself before I go to sleep.'

'You know, if you want to go home to bed, I can look after him,' Beth said, and Hettie nodded.

'Of course you can. And me sleeping here is ridiculous. But that's pretty much how I'm feeling right now. Ridiculous. Indulge me.'

'He's pretty good-looking, isn't he?' Beth said softly, and to her horror Hettie felt herself blush. Blush! She hadn't done such a thing since she was a kid.

'You're talking about Dr Lockhart?'

'Who else would I be talking about? Only the guy you were stranded on the reef with. Who risked his life with you. Also, the guy you've been sitting outside with for an hour.'

'An hour?'

'And five minutes. I timed you. And all the time I thought, he's gorgeous.'

'He's too old to be gorgeous.'

'Are you kidding?'

'He's Caroline's father!'

'And Caroline's twenty-six and her parents were twenty when she was born. That only makes him forty-six.'

'For heaven's sake, after all that's happened today…'

'Especially after what's happened today,' Beth said, becoming serious. 'Honest, Hettie, you do so much for everyone, and now you're talking about adopting Joni…'

'That's not being generous. It's entirely selfish.'

'Maybe, but it's left out a whole chapter of your life. It's called your Love Life. You run this hospital brilliantly,

you watch all your staff have affairs, fall in love, have fun.
But you—'

'Am I or am I not your boss?' Hettie demanded, and
Beth chuckled.

'Yes, you are, ma'am.' And she gave a mock salute. 'But
I've never heard that giving your boss a bit of well-mean-
ing advice is insubordination. Max Lockhart's gorgeous.
I say go for it.'

'Beth…'

'That's all,' Beth said, and stooped and kissed her. So
much for respect, Hettie thought. Beth was an island girl,
born and bred, and she knew everything about this island.
She probably knew far too much about Max Lockhart. 'But,
honest, Hettie, it's been an appalling day and we all know
there's appalling stuff behind that mask you wear. You're
going to fight for Joni? Good for you, but while you're about
it, what about fighting for his uncle, as well? He might be
Ian's brother but to my mind he's *bee-yoo-ti-ful*.'

CHAPTER FIVE

To HIS ANNOYANCE Max slept half the next day. He emerged from his bedroom at noon, feeling disoriented. Weird.

Caroline was in the kitchen, cooking and humming an old island folk tune. For an instant she could have been his mother. The tune was an ingrained part of his childhood, as was the smell of the meal she was cooking.

She turned as he entered, and smiled, and she was his daughter again and time had moved on, but the surge of emotion didn't move with it.

He'd been raised on this island. He loved it. He loved its people. He loved this house.

He'd been away for more than half his life, yet it still felt like home.

'Hey,' Caroline said, and smiled some more.

And he thought, *That was Ellie's smile*. But he could hardly conjure her now. Ellie. His wife.

'Welcome to the world of up,' Caroline said. 'Would you like breakfast or would you like curry? Keanu will be here in ten minutes. I've made his mum's recipe—fish curry with a magnificent red emperor caught this morning. Coconut milk and limes picked an hour ago. There's nothing like it. Oh, and Hettie rang to find out how you were. I asked her for lunch, too, but she's staying with Joni.'

'She still wants to keep him?'

Caroline looked troubled.

'Yes, but I don't see how she can. Keanu's contacted social services. A couple of welfare officers will be on the flight the day after tomorrow. They'll make an interim decision.'

'So soon?'

'If he's to be adopted, the sooner the better. His stepfather doesn't want him.' She eyed her father for a couple of moments and then ventured, 'Unless… Dad, do you want to keep him yourself?'

And there it was, front and centre, and with her words the past slammed back. Standing in the intensive care nursery in a Sydney hospital, with the two tiny scraps of humanity that were his children. He'd been twenty years old, a kid himself. Ellie was dead. The doctor had just spelled out Christopher's probable future.

'How will you care for them?' the doctor had asked, and Max hadn't been able to answer. But he'd muddled through. His parents had suggested taking Caroline home to Wildfire. Christopher had needed specialist care, though, so unless he abandoned him to foster care, Max was stuck on the mainland. His father had agreed to fund him through a medical degree, and somehow he'd cared for Christopher. After Ellie's death, though, he was determined to get a decent medical service for Wildfire, so somehow he'd found time to put pressure on politicians. He'd made noise in the right places and even sent money home to help get the Wildfire hospital up and running.

It had all just been reaction, though. He'd done what had come next. That's what he'd been doing for twenty-six years. Was this another such moment?

'Hey, Dad, don't look like that,' Caroline said softly. 'If Hettie really wants him, we'll support her. Maybe we can organise things so she can. If worst comes to worst, we've

discussed it and Keanu and I will adopt him. No one's forcing Joni on you.'

'No one's forcing anyone.' He shook his head. 'And you
can't adopt a child as worst-case scenario. Sorry, love. Let's
think this through later. Your curry smells great.'

'It does, doesn't it?' Caroline agreed, and then Keanu
arrived, filthy after clearing fallen palms from behind the
hospital. There was cyclone damage to talk over, then the
wedding to discuss and island affairs and arrangements to
be made. The rest of the day passed in a blur and Max had
to put the thought of one small boy aside.

And the thought of the woman who loved him?

Hettie had a busy day at the hospital, followed by another
sleepless night, and then she was faced with something she
would have rather forgotten.

Had she been nuts, suggesting this? It had been an off-
the-cuff suggestion and she was hoping Max had forgotten.
What had she been thinking, suggesting an early morning assignation? A swim below the research station? Why
would he want to do such a thing—and with her?

She should leave a message at the Lockhart place for
him to forget it. Or tell Caroline.

Ha!

'Tell your father I don't want to meet him tomorrow
morning,' she'd say. She could imagine Caroline's reaction.

He would have forgotten, she decided, but if he hadn't...

Okay, if he hadn't then he had a choice. He'd be there or
he wouldn't. It wouldn't worry her either way. She loved
swimming—she swam most mornings. If you blocked out
the fallen trees and mass of leaf litter, the island was at its
gorgeous best and she wasn't on duty today.

But did she want to go swimming with Max?

Who wouldn't? He was...

Gorgeous?

Yes, he was, she told herself, and if she was interested she'd think he was very gorgeous indeed, but she wasn't interested, at least not like that. She was well over such nonsense. She had to be.

But if he happened to be there...

Then they'd have a brisk, businesslike swim, she told herself. Joni was still in the children's ward—Keanu wasn't letting her take him home until after the welfare visit. Caroline was on duty. Bugsy was asleep under his cot. The child welfare visit the next day was looming large and she needed exercise to drive her thoughts from it.

And she reached the fork in the track and Max was sitting on a fallen palm, looking for all the world like he was waiting for her.

But he didn't look like he was heading for a swim. He was dressed almost formally, in chinos and a short-sleeved, open-neck shirt, almost a business shirt. He was wearing brogues, for heaven's sake. He was clean-shaven, smart— no, more than smart.

He was almost breathtakingly good-looking.

She was wearing a sarong and sandals. She'd let her hair cascade to her shoulders.

All of a sudden she felt practically naked. Like she should turn and run?

'I thought you might have forgotten.' He rose and smiled at her, for all the world like he'd been looking forward to this strange assignation.

'I don't...I don't forget appointments.'

'I can see that about you,' he said approvingly. 'Nice sarong.'

'I... Thank you. Neat...shirt.'

'Thank you, too.'

'And brogues?' She couldn't help the note of teasing.

'You know they found my boat?'

She did know. They'd towed it into harbour yesterday.

They'd also found Sefina's body, but Hettie wasn't going there.

'I… Yes.'

'So I have my clothes—and I have an assignation other than the one with you. I hoped we might combine them.'

'Sorry?'

'With the sheikh,' he told her. 'The businessman who's funded the reopening of the research station and the resort. He's invited me for breakfast. I've never met a sheikh. I've only spoken to him on the phone. See me nervous.'

'Hence the brogues.'

'It seems disrespectful to wear sandals.'

'So you're inviting me? With sarong and sandals?'

'Women get latitude. I dare say every woman in his harem wears sarong and sandals.'

'He's not like that,' she said sharply, and he raised his brows.

'You've met him?'

'Sheikh Rahman-al-Taraq? Otherwise known as Harry? Yes, I have. You know he's an oil billionaire? He's also a brilliant paediatric surgeon but a near-fatal brush with encephalitis has left him with hand tremors that prevent him from operating. He's now intent on wiping encephalitis from the face of the planet, which is why he invested here. But you must know that already, and we all know now that your brother conned him into thinking he could buy the land here. We're just so grateful he's bigger than…'

'My shady brother?' Max sighed and fell silent.

They started walking towards the resort, easily, almost with the familiarity of longtime friends. There was still fallen timber on the track. They needed to concentrate on where they walked. A couple of times they faced logs fallen over the path. The first time it happened Max offered his hand to Hettie to help her over.

'You're the one with the cut legs,' she said, and he smiled.

'I'm the one with brogues. Indulge me.'

'I'm fine on my own.'

'Aren't we both,' he said softly, but still he held out his hand. 'Indulge me,' he said again, and there was nothing for it but to put her hand in his and let him support her as she stepped over or through the litter.

It was nothing more than a gentlemanly gesture, she told herself when it happened the second time. It was good old-fashioned courtesy, and why it had the power to make her feel…?

She didn't know how she was feeling.

As if she was almost looking forward to the next fallen log?

Weird.

Focus on practicalities, she told herself, trying hard to block out the feel of Max's hand holding hers. Trying to block out the strength of him, the way he made every nerve ending seem to tingle.

Think of Max, the man. Max, the owner of Wildfire Island, finally about to meet the sheikh who was helping to save it.

For the last couple of years things on the island had been a mess. While Max's son had been gravely ill in Sydney, Max's brother had illegally 'sold' the land and buildings to Sheikh al Taraq. By the time Max had discovered that documents had been signed in his name, the research station had been rebuilt as a state-of-the-art conference centre.

The Sheikh would have been within his rights to walk away and sue for millions. Thanks to Max's frantic phone negotiations, somehow the situation had been saved.

It seemed almost ludicrous now, though, that Max had never met him.

'I've only seen the sheikh in my work gear, though, and

only as a nurse,' Hettie told him. 'Breakfast in my sarong…
You do realise I'm wearing my bikini underneath.'

'Excellent.' Max's magnetic smile flashed out again.
'I'm wearing boxers.'

'Better than the last ones I saw?'

His grin broadened. 'Yes, indeed. I'm almost respectable.'

'As opposed to me.' She tried to glower, which was
hard when his grin made her want to smile back. His grin
seemed to be made for sharing. His grin seemed…almost
dangerous. 'One slip of the tie at my breast and I'm… Well,'
she managed. 'I'll sit still, that's all I'm saying.'

'So you will join us?'

'You'll be wanting to talk business. I can't imagine it's
anything to do with me.'

'I can't imagine there's anything on this island you don't
know about,' Max said gently. 'Support me, Hettie. I need
your strength.'

'You know, I'm very sure you don't.'

'Then you don't know anything about me,' he said, and
suddenly his voice was grim. 'Not many people do.'

The breakfast with the sheikh went brilliantly. They sat
outside the resort's wonderful new restaurant, under the
bougainvillea and frangipani, with brilliantly coloured island parrots squawking in the trees above them and occasionally daring a brave foray to try and filch a sugar
lump. The sheikh—'Call me Harry'—was polite, gentle
and non-accusatory.

'Every family has troubles,' he told Max, when Max
tried to apologise as he'd apologised over and over, via
telephone, via his lawyers. 'And now your brother is dead.
I'm so sorry, but we need to move forward. You know I
invested in this facility to make a difference to the world-
wide scourge of mosquito-borne encephalitis. This is my

passion. I have other facilities around the world but this one is important to me, and Wildfire itself seems to have found its way into my heart.' He smiled. 'You know I've married a woman who loves Wildfire as much as I do? How can I argue with my heart? So now how can we make the best of the situation, for us, for the islanders and for the research-ers who I hope will use this island?'

He then launched into plans that Max found impossible not to engage in. Clinical trials for the encephalitis vaccine were well under way, but meanwhile Harry was offering Max assistance in an insect eradication programme, and in other island medical needs, as well. The two men were soon deep in conversation, and Hettie sat back and listened.

She listened with intelligence, though, Max thought. Through the hour they sat there she asked four questions, each simple but each intensely focussed. She spoke little, but when she did, it was to maximum effect.

It took him little time to realise she already had Harry's respect. She spoke and Harry deferred to her local knowl-edge—and to her intellect.

As she sat, demure and quiet, he found himself more and more drawn to her. She was wearing no make-up. Her curls were free to tumble to her shoulders. The tie of her sarong sat low in the curve of her breasts.

The work he and Harry were talking of was vital. All his attention should be on business, but it was as if there was some magnetic pull, tugging his gaze to that tie.

Hettie looked…almost like a girl.

Except she wasn't. There were life lines around her eyes. Her hands were worn from a career in nursing where she washed them a hundred times a day. And the way she held herself, with quiet dignity…

She was no girl. She was every bit a woman.

'But I'm holding you up.' With their business finished,

the sheikh rose. 'I can see by Hettie's outfit that you're heading for the beach. For the rock pool below the resort?'

'You've taken away the barriers,' Hettie said. 'I assume it's okay?'

'The barriers were only there during construction,' the sheikh told them. And then his voice softened. 'The rock pool where Joni's mother died is a favourite place to swim, as well. I know you swim there, Hettie. I hope you can return to swim there again, but for now please use our pool. I'm so sorry. It's an appalling tragedy and I know this is none of my business, but, Max... The little boy...your nephew... How will you care for him?'

And there it was again.

This little boy is yours.

'The welfare people will be on the island tomorrow,' Max said brusquely. 'They need to assess what's best for him.'

Harry glanced at Hettie. 'My sources say you would take him.'

'I could,' Hettie said, and unconsciously tilted her chin. 'I would. If I'm permitted.'

'You know that isn't an ideal solution.'

'Why not?' Max asked, and Harry cast him a curious glance.

'This is your island. You don't know the mood of the community?'

'Max hasn't spent any time here for years,' Hettie told the sheikh, obtusely defensive on Max's behalf. 'He's been supporting his son in Sydney. He's also been doing everything he can to support the islanders.'

'This I already know.' Harry held up a hand as if in apology for what he had to say. 'But, Max, I also know how your brother has besmirched your name. Your brother was hated. The mine collapse, the death of a beloved island elder... These are only two of the many crimes put to his account.' His voice gentled. 'I've only been on this island a short while, but already I know the stigma the child will carry. And Hettie, as a single mother, you won't be able to protect him from that stigma.'

'I can.' Hettie rose abruptly. 'This isn't the time to discuss it, though. Meanwhile, if you two need to talk more, I'll leave you to it. Max, if you still want a swim, I'll see you in the pool. Otherwise I'll see you back at the hospital.'

She walked out, leaving the two men gazing after her.

But she couldn't disguise her distress. Harry's words had battered her.

'She might be able to care for him,' Max said softly into the stillness that followed, but Harry shook his head.

'The child will be seen as a Lockhart.'

'I'm a Lockhart.'

'Yes. And I understand the situation. Even though your brother was hated, this community still looks to you for leadership. If you stayed…you might afford this child some protection.'

'I'm not staying. I'm here for my daughter's wedding and then I'll leave.'

'To be free?'

'I… Yes.' What was the purpose of denying it? Besides, this man deserved honesty. 'This island killed my wife. I've been away for twenty-six years. The island has little to do with me.'

'And yet you love it.'

'I don't.' It was an angry snap but as he stared out over the sea to the cluster of islands beyond he felt that age-old tug that made a liar of him. And Harry knew.

'How can you not?' Harry shook his head. 'I know. You don't want the mantle of responsibility and yet it's yours regardless. I, too, have responsibilities I can't walk away from. This is your community, and, like it or not, the child, Joni, is your responsibility.'

'Hettie can have him.'

'That's just the problem,' Harry said gently. 'You know and I know that Hettie can't.'

When all else fails, swim. It was a mantra that had held her in good stead all her life. Maybe that was one of the reasons she loved Wildfire. The sea was tropically warm, turquoise waters washed over brilliant coral, and freshwater pools dotted the island. Apart from the occasional storm, she could swim year round.

She needed to swim now. The pool behind the resort was a naturally formed rock pool, fed by waterfalls from the mountains above, with an outlet at the end where the water tumbled to the sea. The water was crystal clear, the rocky bottom dotted with clumps of water grasses. Brilliantly coloured fish darted from clump to clump, but here in this protected place there were no large predators. If she floated she could almost touch the fish with her fingers.

But today Hettie wasn't floating. She put her head down and swam the full length of the rock pool, up and back, up and back. She blocked out everything except the need to expend energy, to get rid of this grey hopelessness that had been with her since she'd seen Sefina walk off the cliff edge.

Or maybe before that. Maybe a long time before. Maybe Joni's helplessness was bringing out emotions she'd suppressed for years.

And with that thought came another. Did she want to adopt Joni for Joni's sake—or for hers?

And then there was the way she was feeling about Max. The way he made her feel...

Like she was a vulnerable kid again. Out of control.

Scared.

Her mind was a kaleidoscope of emotions that swimming couldn't settle. She swam and she swam...

And suddenly Max was swimming with her. Suddenly he was right beside her, pacing her stroke for stroke.

He swam with ease. She was pushing herself but she was aware that his power was constrained. He could lap her if he wished.

He didn't wish. He simply chose to swim beside her.

For a moment she considered stopping, pulling back, telling him to find his own space to swim. But that'd be impolite. Besides, he owned this island. Okay, Harry was leasing this part but she wasn't too sure of landlord rights and she didn't feel up to treading water and telling Max Lockhart to take himself off.

So she kept on swimming and Max kept on pacing her. Stroke for stroke. On and on.

And finally she found herself relaxing, just a little. The tension that had been with her since Sefina's death eased. Her mind was focussing on Max instead, and strangely, thankfully, her irrational fear was fading, as well.

But it was a strange sensation, swimming in tandem with this man. He'd eased his power back so he exactly matched hers. It meant there was no sound apart from the precise, matched strokes. The morning sun was glinting on the water. The fish were darting every which way underneath them and the grasses were swaying lazily as they passed.

It was almost mesmerising. It was…beautiful.

So was the man beside her.

That was dumb. She was trying to make her thoughts practical. Prosaic. She needed to be matter-of-fact about this. She'd invited Max to swim with her this morning and that's what he was doing. Nothing more, nothing less.

So do it.

They swam length after length, diving as they reached the rocks at the ends, tumble-turning and swimming back. Over and over. Not connecting. Simply pacing each other.

Except they were connecting in a way she didn't understand. It was disturbing. It wasn't bad. It wasn't threatening. But it was...disturbing.

She shouldn't have asked him to join her, she decided. She was a loner. Since divorcing Darryn all those years ago, she'd retired into herself. She had friends, she was sociable enough, but she held herself to herself.

Over the past few months there'd been a flurry of romances between the medics on the island, so much so that she was thinking of buying wedding gifts in job lots. But each time she'd watched one of her staff fall in love, a part of her had been flinching. *Be careful*, she'd wanted to warn them. *Fall with your head, not your heart.*

They wouldn't have listened. Hormones had held sway.

And right now hormones were having a fine time with her and she couldn't prevent it. The sensation of Max's body beside her, not touching and yet moving so his strokes matched hers, the rush of water that followed his strokes... It was almost a caress. His body was so large. So male...

And this water wasn't cold enough. She needed to go and find a cold shower—but that'd mean breaking the moment and she couldn't. Whether she willed it or not, she was held in thrall by the sensation of a man she hardly knew swimming beside her.

The sun warmed her body, glinted on the water, glistened on the large male body beside her. This was like a trance, a dream. Soon she'd wake up, but not yet, not yet.

For some reason an illusion crept into her mind and stayed. The illusion that she wasn't alone. Not just here. Not just now. But somehow her customary solitude had been invaded in a way she...wanted?

This was crazy. Her mind was all over the place.

All she could do was keep on swimming.

He hadn't meant to lap with her. At first Max had settled onto a rock at the water's edge. He'd watched Hettie for a while—she really was a wonderful swimmer—and finally he'd stroked out to meet her.

But she hadn't seen him come, and as he'd reached her it had seemed right not to interrupt her solitude. But somehow it had also seemed right to keep swimming, to stroke beside her, and then to match his pace to hers.

Maybe it was an intrusion. If it was, though, surely she'd have raised her head and glared? She knew he was with her. At the last turn she'd fallen a stroke behind. Instead of staying behind, though, she'd raised her stroke rate until once again they'd been in rhythm.

They were swimming as one.

It was almost a kind of lovemaking.

Where had that thought come from? And how crazy was it? This wasn't a woman to make love to. This was Henrietta de Lacey, charge nurse of Wildfire Island hospital. She was practically his employee.

She was not his sort of woman.

Who was…his sort?

No one, he thought as he swam. His one foray into marriage had catapulted him into a catastrophe so great it had overtaken his life. Since then he'd had the occasional relationship but they'd mostly been with colleagues, and all had been on a strict no-future basis. There were many women in medicine who welcomed such friendships. They were career oriented, focussed on getting ahead, knowing a family would interfere with what they wanted in life.

What did he want in life?

Why was he wondering that now, as he stroked back and forth?

Because he hadn't had time to think about it until now? Because there'd never been a choice? Christopher's needs, the island's needs, his daughter…

Now suddenly the future lay ahead like a blank slate. What did he want?

Freedom? Yes!

He swam some more and Hettie swam with him, and he found himself thinking of what Hettie wanted. To take on a child who wasn't her own.

To knowingly step into responsibility.

The thought made him shudder. Freedom had hung before him for twenty-six years, unattainable, a dream he could barely imagine. To give it up...

What was Hettie thinking of?

He shouldn't want to know, he told himself. It was none of his business—as the child she wanted was none of his business.

He should stop swimming alongside her. He should...

No. There was no *should*. He was free. Harry was willing to pour money into the island's medical facilities, making his own small contribution almost unnecessary. Christopher was dead. Caroline was marrying the man of her dreams.

And one little boy? If Hettie wanted that responsibility it was up to her. He could walk away.

Except for now all he wanted was to swim.

They swam for almost an hour and in the end it was Max who called a halt. He reached the flat rock at the end of the pool, and as Hettie turned to do another lap he hauled himself out of the water.

She did another two laps alone. It felt like she'd lost something.

That was fanciful. She'd lost nothing. She'd swum in this pool often since she'd arrived on the island. Sometimes colleagues swam with her but mostly she swam alone.

She didn't mind being alone.

She wouldn't be able to do it with Joni.

Yes, she would. She could teach him to swim. The thought gave her a surge of pleasure, of hope, but it wasn't enough to dispel the weird, desolate sense of losing Max's presence beside her.

Wow, she was being dumb. She had no right to be thinking like this.

Right? That was the wrong word, she decided. She had no *desire* to be thinking like that.

Desire. There was a loaded word.

She shook it off, almost with anger. She finished another lap.

If she kept swimming, would Max go away? How ungracious was that? She slowed, reached the rocks and pulled herself out.

The rocks were slippery. Max's hand came out and caught her wrist. She was tugged up, faster than she expected, a little closer than she expected.

He was so...male. He must spend serious time in the gym, she thought tangentially. A twenty-year-old would kill for Max's body.

A twenty-year-old could never have this body. Wet, clad only in board shorts, his silver-shot black hair dripping, rivulets of water running down his bare chest, he looked...

Distinguished?

It was the wrong word but she was too close to him to think of another.

Mature. Strong.

Very, very sexy.

Whoa...

'That was some swim,' he said, and smiled at her, and that smile was almost her undoing. How could a guy's smile light up his face? More. How could it light up...something inside her she didn't know had been dark?

He'd tugged her up on the rocks to sit beside him. Mosses covered the surface. The sun was warm on her face. The moss was as soft as bedding, and this man beside her was so...

Near.

She should edge away. She couldn't. Her body wouldn't move.

'You're some swimmer,' he said, and she tried smiling herself. She wasn't sure it came off.

'You're not so bad yourself. Not many men can keep up with me.'

'I can see that about you.' One of her curls had flopped over her eye. He leaned forward and tucked it behind her ear.

'Th-thank you.'

'My pleasure.' His voice was deep and resonant, almost a caress on its own. 'So…no men in your life?'

'Is this a come-on?'

'It's not.' His smile lit his face again. 'Not that I'm not interested…'

'Don't do that,' she snapped, and his smile died.

'What?'

'You sound like your brother.'

That produced a sharp intake of breath—and instant anger. 'You'd judge me like Ian?'

She hesitated. 'No,' she said at last. 'That's not fair. But you look like him.'

'And he…came on?'

'He tried,' she said darkly. 'He regretted it. He also tried messing with a couple of my nurses. He regretted that, too.'

'That sounds scary.'

'I invoked you,' she told him, and lightened up a little, remembering a late-night conversation when she'd found Ian propositioning one of her very young ward assistants. 'Rumours were that you didn't know half the stuff Ian did, so I told him that if he messed with my staff I'd personally fly to Sydney and lay every folly I knew about him in front of you. I said it once in desperation, and to my astonishment he backed off. After that I only had to glare at him.'

'He was scared of me?' Max said incredulously.

'I believe he was afraid of you finding out what a toerag he was.'

'I wish you *had* told me.'

'You had enough to worry about,' she said gently. 'That was the island consensus. We knew how ill Christopher was. I'm glad we didn't worry you.'

'But if you had...'

'No.' And this time it was her turn to touch him. His face had grown grim. She could see the pain of remembrance, of regret, and she couldn't help herself. She reached out and traced the strong contours of his face, a feather touch, a touch of comfort and nothing more. 'Max, you've done all you can for this island. To stop Ian you would have had to leave Christopher, and that would have been unthinkable. Your first care had to be for your son.'

'As your first care will be?'

'If I'm allowed to keep Joni, yes.'

'You'll make a formidable mother.'

'Don't you believe it,' she said, suddenly feeling shaky. 'I'm tough on the outside but I'm squishy in the middle.'

'Which is the best combination for a mum.'

'You think so?'

'I know so.' His hand came up and caught hers. 'Hettie, you know it'll be hard.'

'It'll be hard but it'll be fun.' She should pull away from his touch, she thought. His hand was holding hers and it was totally inappropriate, but to pull away seemed...ungracious?

Impolite?

Unthinkable.

'It might not happen,' Max warned.

'I know that. But I will fight for it.'

'You have no one to help you.'

'I won't need help. Like you, I've learned to be independent.'

'I don't see Child Welfare seeing independence as an attribute.'

'Strength must be.' She looked down at their linked hands. Once more she thought about pulling away, but once more came the realisation that pulling away was impossible.

'I hope you're right.' He, too, was looking at their linked hands and his face twisted into a wry, self-mocking smile. 'Strength has to be fed, though.'

'So how did you stay strong? All those years?'

'I'm not sure I did,' he confessed. 'Maybe on the outside…'

'I guess that's the important part. The part we show to the world.'

'That's the part you'll show to Child Welfare when they assess you?'

'What else should I show them?'

'Maybe the softer bits,' he suggested.

'Softer?'

'The distress you feel at Sefina's death. The regret. And the way Joni makes you feel…'

'How do you know how he makes me feel?'

'I had twins, remember?' he said gently. 'I was twenty years old, I was grief-stricken, I was terrified, and I held them and knew I'd do anything in my power to protect them. It was enough to make me study medicine, to make me vow to learn everything I could for Christopher. It was even enough for me to send Caroline back to the island to live with my parents and my aunt. I loved her enough to let her go.'

There was a long silence at that.

Their hands were still linked. It *was* inappropriate, Hettie thought inconsequentially, and everything seemed inconsequential just now.

Everything except that link.

But somewhere in that conversation was something she had to pursue. A warning?

'Are you saying...maybe I should let Joni go?' she asked into the stillness, and he didn't answer for a while. His fingers started massaging hers. It was a comfort touch, maybe something he'd learned to do for Christopher, she thought, but it didn't feel like something he'd do for Christopher.

Or maybe it was just that she was a woman and he was every bit a man...

A man who was too close.

A man to whom she wouldn't mind being closer.

'I don't know,' Max said at last, heavily now, still massaging her fingers, using his thumb and middle finger to knead their length, strong, firm, sure. 'I only know you're offering something I can't. To commit... Hettie, it's for a lifetime.'

'That's what I want.'

'I've done a lifetime.' His words were suddenly angry. She flinched. He closed his eyes and shook his head. 'I'm sorry.' He released her hand, then absently lifted the other and started massaging again. She had a sudden image of Max, a surgeon, always on call, finding time every day to be at his son's bedside, gently working his magic.

For a lifetime...

'You can't regret,' she whispered, and he shook his head.

'No. Except the time I couldn't spend with Caroline.'

'Caroline understands.'

'Will Joni understand that you need to work?'

'Other women work when they're on their own.'

'So do men, as I did, but believe me it's usually not by choice. Sole parenthood is just plain hard.'

'So if they ask—Child Welfare—will you support me?'

'Why would you need my support?'

'You're his uncle. His legal guardian. Your wishes should make a difference.'

There was a long pause.

'Why do you want him?'

And what did she say to that? She hardly knew herself.

She thought of all the things she should say, the logical arguments she'd already lined up for the welfare people. How she had a secure job, a supportive community. How she already knew Joni and he seemed to trust her. How she'd been a friend of Sefina's, and how, with her, Joni would grow up knowing his background, his heritage. How she'd raise him with love and with all the skill her nursing background could give her.

But that didn't answer Max's question.

Why do you want him?

And there was no answer to that other than the truth.

'I don't know,' she confessed. 'I know I can't have children. Yes, I lost my baby and I mourned, but then I got on with life. My work satisfies me. I love caring for people. I've loved caring for Joni. And yet I've cared for many children without wanting them.'

'But you want Joni.'

'All I know is that when you handed him to me in the water, something changed,' she whispered. 'I held him to me and I wouldn't have let go, even if the rip had carried us both out. Something just…stuck. It was suddenly like he was part of me. Keanu's sent me away now. He says I shouldn't take on all the caring because it'll hurt more when…*if* I have to give him up. But it can't hurt more than it'll hurt right now. Because in that moment…' She shook her head. 'I'm sorry. It doesn't make sense.'

'But it does,' he said gently. 'At twenty years old I held my twins and that was how I felt.'

'They were yours. Their mother was your wife. It did make sense.'

'I don't think sense comes into loving.'

'No,' she said bleakly, 'it doesn't. But Keanu's right. My chances of keeping him...'

'Hettie, I will support you. I will ask that you be allowed to keep him. I can't do more than that, but I'll do my best.'

She closed her eyes. Swallows were swooping across the pool. It was so quiet she could hear their wingbeats as they fluttered back and forth, snatching insects above the water.

Joni wasn't hers yet—but this man would help her.

'Thank you,' she whispered, and he put a hand under her chin and lifted her face and waited until her eyes were open.

'You'll make a good mother,' he told her. 'You're a good person, Hettie. You deserve...'

'I don't deserve...'

'Okay, maybe "deserve" is the wrong word. But you long for a family. I'm over family. I'm free, so holding on to Joni would hold me down. But you... You'll give him all the love he needs. I know you will.'

'How can you know that?' She shouldn't ask, she thought. He'd given her the assurance she wanted. Why ask for more? But the question was out there.

'Because you're you,' he said, and she looked into his eyes and the combination was too much. The stress of the last two days, the tragedy, the shared danger. The shared worry for a small boy. The swim this morning, the sun, the gentle lapping of the water, the sound of the birds...

Whether she raised her face still more, or whether he bent to her, she could never afterwards remember. All she knew was that he was cupping her face. She was moving those last few inches.

And he was kissing her.

CHAPTER SIX

HE HADN'T MEANT to kiss her. Why should he? There was nothing between them. There could be nothing.

His life had just stopped being complicated, and he needed another complication like a hole in the head. He did not need to have an affair with the woman who wanted to adopt his nephew.

But she wasn't just the woman who wanted to adopt his nephew. She was Hettie, a woman who'd risked her life trying to help him, a woman of strength and character, a woman of past tragedy and determination born of that tragedy.

Or...she was none of those things. She was a nymph, a water creature who'd swum beside him, a desirable, beautiful woman.

She was wearing a sliver of a crimson bikini. She was wet but sun-warmed. Her curls were tumbling, still dripping, in tendrils, to her shoulders.

Her eyes were a deep green, slightly shadowed as though she hadn't slept. She had crinkly life lines at the corners of her eyes... Smile lines?

Which brought him to her mouth...

Yeah, it was her mouth where the trouble was. Her lips were full, her mouth was slightly open and his whole consciousness centred on it.

When her face tilted to his, when he drew her to him and he touched her...

When he tasted...

It was an explosion of senses that almost blew him away.

He'd had women—of course he had—lovers as well as friends. A widower was sexy, he'd discovered early. It evoked a nice mix of availability, sympathy and, for some reason, intrigue. It was much sexier than a divorcée. More reliable, too.

Or maybe it was Christopher who evoked the reliability response. Christopher had been his out, but, then, he'd never really needed an out. He'd never let himself get close enough.

I have a disabled son...

He'd used it in his head more than he'd used it out loud. It stopped him getting close. He didn't want to get close.

He was close now. He was so close his brain was in danger of shorting out. Hettie's body was against his, wet and sun-warmed and soft and curvaceous. Her slip of a bikini was barely there. Her mouth was lush under his, and she was taking as well as giving.

This kiss was blowing his mind.

When had a kiss ever tasted like this? When had a woman ever felt like this?

She was ordinary! She was a thirty-something charge nurse, a career medic, someone employed in the hospital he helped fund. She was sensible, determined, capable.

She had no right to be making him feel...

Like this kiss had to be deepened. Like he needed to hold her tighter and tighter still, until her breasts were crushed against his chest and until it felt as if their bodies were melting into each other. Becoming one. He heard a whisper of a moan. Her hands were clutching the small of his back, tugging him as close as he wanted to tug her.

The sea grasses were soft. This place seemed deserted. They could...

'No.'

And suddenly she was pulling away.

The world somehow steadied. Or sort of steadied.

Thank heaven she had some sense, he told himself, because he seemed to have lost his.

He had still lost it. She'd pushed back from him, but her gaze was still locked to his. She was breathing too fast. She put a hand to her heart as if to try and control its beating.

Control. That was what they both needed. This was madness.

'This is crazy.' It was a whisper, words he could barely hear, but behind the whisper he suddenly heard...fear.

What was she afraid of?

And then the image of his brother flashed into his mind. *Anything in a skirt...*

'I'm not like Ian.' If she could think that...

'I know.' Her voice wobbled. 'It's just...'

She couldn't explain further but the moment was shattered. How could she be fearful? Her fear made him feel ill.

'You don't trust me and why should you?' He snagged her sarong from the rocks and tossed it to her, then watched as she tugged it round herself like a shield. She was shaking. Because he'd kissed her?

What sort of damage had his oaf of a brother done on this island?

He was a Lockhart. He couldn't escape that. His neglect had caused grief and heartache for the islanders. Was it now causing this woman to back away?

'I'm sorry.' She had herself under control now, and she even managed a weak smile. 'Whew. That was some kiss.'

'But I'm not Ian.' It was all he could think of to say.

'I know you're not.' But still her voice trembled.

'That kiss,' he said slowly into the silence, 'was not a

kiss of seduction. Neither was it a kiss that said I'll kiss anything in a skirt. Or in your case—' he managed a smile himself '—anything in a bikini.'

'I know you're not like Ian. Of course I do. But it didn't mean anything,' she whispered. And then she took a deep breath, hauling herself together. 'Sorry. I'm not usually a wimp. It's just… I'm usually in control. That feeling…okay, it scared me. Max, I'm not in the market for a relationship, and I don't think you are, either.'

'I'm not.' He had to be blunt. 'I'll be leaving the island after Caroline's wedding. Harry has the research station under control. The mine's being made safe and will be running as a co-operative from now on, and Caroline and Keanu are happy to oversee things. If I need to, I'll come back, but only for fleeting visits.'

'Can I ask why?'

'My wife died here.'

'That seems a bit…excessive.'

'It does, doesn't it?' He shrugged. 'I can't help that. My father brought me up to be the lord of the island, Lord Lockhart, if you like. Dad never had a title but he acted like he did, as did my grandfather before him. I rebelled. I insisted on heading to Australia to university. Then I met Ellie and brought her here and she died.'

'Which was the end of your freedom,' she ventured, and he shrugged.

'What do you think? Dad wanted me to put Christopher in a home. He insisted the island needed me. In my conceit I thought medicine needed me more. Christopher needed me more. And I was right. My grandfather set up a trust for the islanders' medical care but it wasn't enough for a hospital. With me on the ground in Australia, and with my medical knowledge, I was able to badger the authorities into proper funding, and for years now my income has augmented the terrific service you provide. But the choice

I made had costs, so much so that even stepping on the is-land fills me with regret. So now? I'll see Caroline married, and then I'll go back to work. I still command an exorbitant salary so I can still feed funds here. But Harry is promising to help so the load is lessening. Now, in my spare time...'

'You'll be free?'

'Yes.' He said it with vehemence. 'What's wrong with that?'

'Nothing, if it makes you happy.'

'It will.'

'Be careful what you wish for,' she said softly, and looked out over the sunlit water and smiled. Her smile wasn't for him, though. It was a smile filled with sadness, filled with the same regret he was feeling. A smile that looked back over the years and saw...nothing.

Enough. What was he doing here with this woman? She stirred things up in him he had no wish to be stirred. He needed to get back to the house.

Back to...what?

'You had Christopher,' she said gently. 'You loved him. And you have Caroline.'

'I've let her down...'

'It doesn't matter what you have or haven't done in the past,' she snapped, suddenly angry. 'It's what you do today and tomorrow that counts. I can't see running away as an option.'

'I'm not running. No one needs me.'

'Joni...'

'Has you.'

'What if I'm not allowed to adopt him?'

'Then he'll go to adoptive parents in Australia who'll love him. He'll get over this awfulness and so will you.'

'And I'll be free again,' she said in a strange voice, and he couldn't bear it. He wanted to kiss her again. He needed to kiss her.

But she was backing away even more, slipping her feet into her sandals, fastening her sarong tighter.

'I need to get back to the hospital. Joni might be awake. I don't want to leave him for too long.'

'You might have to leave him forever.'

'So why would you care?' she snapped. 'You think freedom's so great? You might even think it's a good thing for me to be alone again.'

'Hettie…'

'No. I didn't say that.' She bit her lip. 'I have a great life. I'm perfectly happy. I don't need Joni. And I don't need you, either, Max Lockhart, which is just as well, seeing you're flying in and flying out. So you can just keep your hands and your mouth to yourself while you're here.'

'You liked kissing me.'

'What if I did?' she snapped. 'I have very poor choice in men.'

And with that she turned and stalked away, leaving him to follow if he wished.

He decided…maybe he shouldn't follow.

Joni was awake when Hettie reached the hospital. She hadn't stopped for a shower or to change. For some reason she felt deeply unsettled.

She needed to ground herself.

But if she needed Joni to ground herself, then she was in trouble. She knew it but she couldn't help herself. She headed for the children's ward and Caroline was sitting beside Joni's cot. She had him out of the cot and was cuddling him, but the little boy was asleep.

'Hey,' she said as Hettie walked in. 'What's up?' Her eyes widened as she saw what Hettie was wearing. Hettie was nothing if not proper in the way she dressed for work.

'I just thought I'd drop by and see how he's doing,' Hettie said defensively.

'I'm not talking about the sarong,' Caroline said gently. 'I'm talking about your face. What's wrong?'

'Nothing.'

'Liar, liar, pants on fire. Hettie, I've only worked with you for three months so I still don't know you very well, but I do know enough to recognise trouble.'

'Your dad...' Hettie said, before she could stop herself, and Caroline's face stilled.

'What about my dad?'

'I...' Hettie shook her head. 'Sorry. Nothing. I was just talking to him...'

'In bathers and a sarong?'

'He was telling me...' She fought for a minute for composure. What if she really said what had happened? That Max had kissed her until her toes had curled, that he'd made her feel as young and vulnerable as a teenager, and she'd felt so out of control she was terrified? Um...not.

'He'll support me if I want to keep Joni,' she managed.

'But he doesn't think it will happen?'

'I think he thinks it's a whim.'

'It's not?'

'No.'

'But you're not family.' Caroline looked down at the little boy in her arms. 'He's my family. My uncle's child. My cousin.'

'Do you want him?'

'N-no,' Caroline told her. 'Is that selfish? But if no one else will...'

'He'll be adopted in Australia. It's sensible.'

'Yeah,' Caroline muttered. 'Sensible. Like Dad sending his daughter back to Wildfire while he stayed in Australia. Sensible.'

'Did he have a choice?'

'No,' Caroline conceded. 'But it did hurt, no matter how

much I reassure Dad. And it'll hurt Joni. He should stay here. I'll talk to Dad. See if he can apply more pressure...'

'He's said he'll support me,' Hettie said again, and Caroline's eyes frowned.

'Is there something between...?'

'No!'

'There is! Hettie... You and Dad?'

'There's nothing!'

But Caroline's eyes had lit with excitement. 'Hettie, that'd be awesome. You and Dad and Joni...'

'Caro, cut it out. It was one kiss.'

'He kissed you? My dad kissed you?'

'That makes me feel about eighty. Stop it.'

'It shouldn't make you feel eighty. Dad's gorgeous. Oh, Hettie... You could make him stay here. He could take on work at the hospital—heaven knows, the islands could use a full-time surgeon. You could be a family. Hettie, this is amazing. We just have to get it sorted before the welfare people arrive...'

'Will you stop it?' Hettie was half angry, half laughing. 'Of all the ridiculous... One kiss doesn't make a romance.'

'No, but the way you're looking...I know a romance when I see one. Oh, it'd be so wonderful for both of you.'

'Caro, don't.' The laughter faded. She looked down at the little boy in Caroline's arms and she felt...ill.

And Caro's teasing faded. She looked up at Hettie for a long moment and then she rose and gently lowered Joni back into his cot.

'I won't,' she said softly. 'It's just...it would be so perfect. Why did he kiss you?'

'Heaven knows. He's a Lockhart?'

'That's unfair,' Caroline told her. 'As far as I know, Dad hasn't had a single serious affair since Mum died. I asked him once when I was a kid when he was getting married again. You know what he said? He said he had his family.

He'd married my mother, he had Christopher and me, and we were all the family he ever needed. Only you know what? From here, with Chris gone and Mum gone and me marrying Keanu, his family's looking a bit lean. But I'd imagine he's still not even thinking about anything serious. Twenty-six years...maybe he's out of the habit.'

'That's none of my business.'

'It's not, is it?' Caroline said seriously. 'But, oh, Hettie, wouldn't it be great if it was?'

Sam, the island's medical director, arrived back later that morning, and he strode from the plane looking immensely pleased with himself. Apparently the patient he'd escorted to the mainland was on the way to full recovery. There was also a woman, Caroline told Max, a paramedic called Lia whom Sam had hoped to see in Brisbane. His grin said that he had seen her, and his love life was just fine.

His grin got even broader when he learned that Max was back. 'Great to have you here, sir,' he told him, and they celebrated by going through the hospital finances. Maybe both men wanted to be thinking of other things but it had to be done. Ian had managed to bleed funds from the hospital, but not enough to cause significant problems. Max's job was to figure out where the gaps were and plug them.

There was also the damage done by the cyclone. There'd been a power surge, and the CT scanner was damaged. A leak had also caused problems behind the kitchen stoves and one of the wards was unusable.

He needed to get back to the mainland and start working again, he thought. He couldn't ask Harry to donate for general maintenance.

Some things he was still responsible for.

'I'm sure Harry would help with this if we asked him,' Sam said as they reached the end of the bookwork. 'If he was allowed. You know he's a doctor himself, a surgeon and a good one. Encephalitis damaged the nerves in his hands so he can no longer operate but he appreciates what we're doing and supports us to the hilt.' He hesitated. 'Speaking of surgeons...I have an islander with suspected appendicitis in room three. Our only surgeon, Sarah, is currently completing her fly in, fly out roster—did you know she and Harry have just married? But at the moment she's on the mainland. Tomas seems to be settling, but if he flares in the night can I call on you?'

'Of course. You'd normally fly him out?'

'Keanu and I can cope with a simple appendix, which is what this looks like, but Tomas is in his sixties. With the CT scanner out of action I'd like to send him to the mainland. I'm all for avoiding surprises when we open things up, but the islanders hate leaving.' He hesitated. 'Max, there are many things we could use a specialist surgeon for. At the moment we have Sarah for one week a month but it's not enough and now she's married Harry. Harry loves this place but he has his own country. He has research facilities elsewhere and Sarah will travel with him.'

'You're telling me the position's vacant.'

'Interested?'

'For tonight, yes.'

'But not forever?'

'A week and then I'm gone.'

'You hate it here so much?'

Max hesitated. Did he hate the island?

No. He loved it. The island was like a siren song, calling him home.

The problem was, though, he'd never been able to see it as home. He saw it as responsibility.

When he'd been born his grandfather had still been alive. He had vague memories of walking with the old man, hand in hand, as old Henry Lockhart had started the process of handing over.

'You'll own this,' he'd said. 'You'll own every square inch, but don't you dare waste it. And don't think of it as pleasure. It's a burden, boy, a sacred trust. My grandfather bought this island and what he didn't realise was that buying it meant responsibility for every islander who makes their living from it. These are your people, Max, boy. You'll work for them for the rest of your life.'

Even then—aged, what, about six?—Max had felt the burden of responsibility. As a kid, roaming the island with the island kids who were his friends, he'd already felt it. If anything happened to his mates, his family and their families, had looked to Max. He remembered his best mate, Rami, falling from the cliffs while they'd been checking birds' nests. Rami had broken his leg. Max's father had belted Max and then sent him to Rami's family to apologise.

'You're a Lockhart,' he'd growled. 'Your responsibility is to keep people safe, not put them in danger.'

Keep people safe...

That's what he'd been juggling all his life. Keeping his children safe. Keeping the islanders safe.

If he allowed Harry to fully fund the hospital... To finally walk away...

'This is your home, isn't it?' Sam asked curiously, and Max dug his hands into his pockets and thought about it.

'I don't do...home,' he said at last. 'When I was in Sydney with Christopher I always thought I should be here. When I was here, Christopher needed me. Home has always meant...guilt.'

'Hell, Max.'

'I'd been thinking I might take a break. I thought I might take *Lillyanna* and sail round the world.' He was attempting lightness he wasn't feeling. 'Until she rolled. The night of the cyclone put me off like you wouldn't believe.'

'I can imagine it would.' Sam hesitated. 'But if you did decide to settle... We might not need your money anymore but your presence would be a godsend. The islanders need a figurehead. Persuading them to get their kids vaccinated. Mosquito eradication. Disease control. So many things... They still look up to you.'

'Even after Ian?'

'Especially after Ian. They knew he was the wrong Lockhart. And, Max...'

'Yes?' He was starting to feel...goaded.

'Hettie and Joni.'

'What about Hettie and Joni?'

'Joni's Ian's son and the islanders treat him as that. If you stayed...he'd be your son. The difference would be unimaginable.'

'I can't take on another family.'

'No one's asking you to take on another family,' Sam said gently.

'But you are pressuring me.'

'I'm just telling you the truth.'

Hettie was on duty that afternoon and she was busy. All she wanted was to be in the children's ward with Joni, but Joni was happy, playing with Leah, the ward clerk, and the hospital seemed suddenly to be full of acute patients who needed her skills.

Tomas Cody was one of them. Sam had examined him and given him pain relief but Tomas wasn't settling and was obviously afraid.

By late afternoon Hettie was thinking of calling Sam back, just to reassure him, but before she could, Max appeared.

He was dressed semi-formally again, and he carried a stethoscope. He paused at Tomas's door and smiled at her.

'Good afternoon, Nurse. Good afternoon, Mr Cody. Dr Taylor's asked me to see you, Mr Cody, in my capacity as a surgeon. Do you know who I am? Max Lockhart...'

'I know who you are,' Tomas muttered. 'Damned Lockhart who ran away...' And then he paused and seemed to regroup. 'Nope, that's wrong. You've been the one sending money, I know that. Keeping this place going. It's your brother who was the bad egg. Blasted pain's got me confused.'

'That's why I'm here,' Max said gently. 'Dr Taylor—Sam—suspects appendicitis. He could send you to the mainland tomorrow but if it is appendicitis I could whip it out here. That is, if you trust me.'

'Of course I trust you. Your mother used to say you'd made a brilliant surgeon. If you can stop this gut ache I'd be grateful.'

'It's okay to examine you?'

'Be my guest.'

So Hettie watched as Max gently questioned, gently examined, gently probed. His questions said he'd confronted this situation hundreds of times before. His very assurance as he performed the examination had Tomas relaxing. Pain could often be augmented by fear, Hettie knew, and somehow Max's very assurance was taking the fear out of it.

And at the end of the examination Max sat by Tomas's bed as if he was prepared to chat.

How many surgeons did that? Hettie thought in astonishment. In her experience surgeons arrived, did a fast examination and then left to discuss the outcome with the lower orders. Not with the patients themselves, at least not first off.

'I think it is appendicitis,' Max told him. 'You have a tender abdomen and a slight temperature, but I can't be sure without a CT scan. Sadly our CT scanner is out of order. It was damaged by a power surge during the cyclone.'

'I don't want to go to the mainland,' Tomas said, startled. 'Not for just an appendix.'

'Well, here's the thing.' Max glanced up at Hettie, a single glance that somehow encompassed her, that told Tomas that Max was part of a medical team, working for the best for him. How did he do that? Hettie wondered. She didn't know. All she knew was that this man engendered trust. It seemed to ooze from him like radio waves, encompassing all in range. 'You're older than most people who present with appendicitis. There's a slight chance you could have some kind of bowel blockage, something that might have caused your appendix to get inflamed. You don't seem very sick so I doubt if that's the case, but it might be. Without a CT scan I can't guarantee it.'

There was a long silence while Tomas took that on board. 'I guess...' He hesitated but then forged on. 'You're saying... Guys of my age... You're saying things can go wrong, huh? If it was a kid with a bad appendix, you'd just think it was their appendix, but with me...well, there's all the C-word stuff. You're saying there's a chance it's cancer?'

He'd repeated what Max had told him in terms of acceptance. How had Max done that? Hettie thought. More and more, she thought, this man had skills that were needed here.

If he could stay...

He wasn't staying, and it was just as well, she reminded herself. After that kiss...

'The chance is small,' Max said. 'But we can't exclude it.'

'So if you operated...' Once more Tomas hesitated and then he forged on. 'If there is something in there, you could fix it?'

'I could try.'

'No promises, right?'

'There never are in medicine,' Max told him, and once more Hettie was stunned by Max's skill in telling it like it was.

'So if I went to the mainland and they did one of those CT scan things and it told them there was cancer...'

How hard had that been to say? Hettie thought, but Max didn't react. It was like cancer was just like a normal word. A non-scary word. A workaday word.

'If I was in Cairns,' Tomas forged on. 'If it was cancer... Someone like you would do the operation, right?'

'That's right.'

'And you'd cope with what's in there when you found it.'

'We'd have a better idea of what we were dealing with,' Max told him. 'We might be better prepared but, yes, it'd be someone like me doing the operating.'

'So you can operate here?'

'I can,' Max said steadily. 'If you trust me. But, Tomas, remember, there's still a very good chance it's just appendicitis.'

But Tomas had relaxed, Hettie thought. The big man had straightened in the bed and was looking directly at Max, man to man. It was like saying the word 'cancer' out loud had brought the bogeyman out in the open where it could be fought, not just by Tomas but by all of them as a team.

'I trust you, Doc,' Tomas said, and Max grinned and reached for his hand to shake it.

'I'm glad to hear it. After so long off the island...'

'You're a real Lockhart,' Tomas muttered. 'Not like the other one. Now, about this gut ache...'

'I'll do something about that right now,' Max said. 'Nurse de Lacey...'

'Hettie,' Tomas growled. 'She's one of us. Our Hettie.'

And what was there in that that made Max flinch? Hettie saw the brief flash of bleakness, but then it was gone.

'Hettie,' Max corrected himself, and he smiled at her, and there it was again, that smile, and why it had the power to disconcert her so much she didn't have a clue. 'I'll write Mr Cody up for—'

'Tomas,' Tomas growled, and Max grinned.

'Only if I'm Max.'

'You're Mr Lockhart,' Tomas growled. 'Some things don't change. Some things shouldn't change. We've needed a Lockhart to be in charge here forever.'

Max's smile faded. He stood looking down at Tomas for a long, long moment and finally he nodded.

'I'll see what I can do,' he said. 'But, meanwhile, we'll give you painkillers and let you sleep. Sam's started you on antibiotics and there's still a good chance things will settle down. But if nothing's changed in the morning then we'll go in and fix things.'

'That's exactly what this island needs,' Tomas muttered. 'Finally, a Lockhart who can fix things.'

Max had dinner at the resort that night. He spent time with Harry, discussing out how to keep the islands, Wildfire and the rest of the M'Langi group, safe into the future.

Yes, Harry was prepared to put funds into the hospital. Yes, there were good men prepared to oversee the mine. Yes, the mosquito eradication and the vaccination programmes could go ahead.

Things were under control. There was no need for Max to stay after Caroline's wedding.

He walked home—no, he walked back to the homestead—late. He walked around the lagoon and then he paused. Hettie was where she'd been that first night he'd sat with her. Looking out over the lagoon.

He paused, and decided not to intrude. He could sense her need for space even from where he was.

There'd been a burial service for Sefina late that afternoon. He'd stood in the background then, too, hating to intrude.

It had been a simple island service with less than a dozen people in attendance. Hettie had stood at the graveside with a couple of the nurses from the hospital. She'd held Joni, and she'd placed a spray of frangipani on the grave. Sefina's son and Sefina's friend saying goodbye.

A part of him had ached to go and stand by them, but he had no right. It wasn't his place. His brother had done such harm...

Some of the island women watched from the background as well, as if, like him, they were ashamed.

In time these women could support Hettie, he thought, if she was allowed to keep Joni. The anger and resentment of Sefina's husband had driven them away, but maybe the fact that Joni was Ian's son could eventually be forgotten.

That had been a moment of hope amid the bleakness, but there seemed only bleakness now.

Hettie was still in her nurse's uniform. She must have just come off duty. She didn't have Joni with her. She was simply staring out over the moonlit water.

He could feel her desolation.

He'd only known her for three days. How did he feel he knew her so well?

Shared experience? They'd been through grief, but hers had been the bleaker harvest. He'd been left with two children. Despite his appalling medical problems, Christopher had brought him joy. Caroline would continue to bring him joy. Hettie had none of that.

In time Caroline and Keanu could even give him grandkids. That was a sudden blindside. Surely he was too young to be a grandfather, but the thought was...amazing. He'd have to come home for that.

Home?

This wasn't home.

Nowhere was home.

He stood on, in the shadows of the palms, and watched Hettie for a few moments more, careful not to make a move, not wanting to intrude. Was he being a stalker, just watching? The thought crossed his mind, but he pushed it away. He needed this time to watch her.

She seemed so bereft. So alone.

Sam seemed to think the authorities would come down hard on her wish to keep Joni. Maybe she was mourning that already, as she was mourning the death of her friend. But Hettie must've known more than most that she could survive grief and move on.

But did she need to?

An image flashed into his mind, a tiny nebulous thought. A thought so ridiculous…

He and Hettie and Joni. A family. They'd let Joni stay then.

A family. Was he out of his mind? This was tiredness speaking, he decided, and grief, and a bit of shock and pain thrown in for good measure.

Enough. He could justify watching her no longer. He turned and slipped away, aware as he did so of a sharp stab of loss.

Like leaving part of him behind?

No!

He was still raw from Christopher's death, he told himself. He was in no state to be thinking of anything other than the needs of himself, his daughter and the island.

So why were the needs of one nurse suddenly so important?

Why, when he went to bed, did he lie awake and think of Hettie?

Why did the faint idea of family suddenly seem possible?

How did she know he was there?

She had no idea. It was like a sixth sense, telling her there was someone among the shadows.

Maybe she should be nervous. Maybe she should be creeped out.

She wasn't. It was Max. She knew it, and she also knew he was fighting shadows that were as long as her own.

She didn't move. She didn't by as much as a blink let on that she knew he was there. There was no need, for it seemed he was doing the same as she was.

He'd be looking into the future and seeing only echoes of the past.

This was dumb. She was tired and she had to be at her best tomorrow. She had to make a good impression on the welfare people. More, she had to convince them she could be mother and father to Joni and that she could care for him better than some adoptive parents in Australia.

Could she?

It was too huge a question for her to answer.

Max would support her. The thought was comforting but strangely it wasn't enough.

She wanted more. From Max?

Why was she thinking that? She had no right.

'Enough.' She said it out loud, knowing, once again without understanding how, that Max had gone, and the night felt emptier for his going.

CHAPTER SEVEN

TOMAS WAS NO better the next morning. The drugs Max had prescribed had had to be topped up in the small hours and when Max saw him at eight, he was starting to slip into an abyss of pain.

'Enough,' Max told him. 'If it's okay with you, Tomas, we're going in. I'll operate. Sam will do the anaesthetic.'

'And Hettie will be there, too?' Tomas demanded. Hettie had come into the ward with Max and was standing at his side, waiting for orders.

'I'm not much use,' Hettie told him. 'I just get to stand around and watch the doctors do their thing.'

'Yeah,' Tomas growled. 'Like we know that's true. There's no one on this island we'd rather have than Hettie in an emergency,' he told Max. 'We're limited in doctors. The number of times she's had to step in, stitch people up, help mums with bubs, cope until a doc can get here... She ought to be a doctor, our Het. Some of us reckon she already is.'

'Hush,' Hettie told him. 'Don't give him any ideas. If you think it's fun to chop people open...'

'I reckon you could do it if you had to,' Tomas said stubbornly, and Max glanced at Hettie and saw her blush, and thought he wouldn't be the least bit surprised if Tomas was right.

'So you want Hettie there in case Sam or I fall over?' he asked, and Tomas managed a weak grin.

'That's the one. With Hettie I know nothing will go wrong.'

She's that sort of woman, Max thought. Though the weird fantasies of last night had slipped back where they belonged, into the realms of tired night dreams that could be safely ignored, it still gave him curious comfort to think that when he left the island Hettie would stay on. It was as if the island was safe in her hands.

His daughter intended to stay here. Maybe in time Hettie could even deliver her babies. She could be here for her.

As he couldn't? Because he could no longer do family?

Enough. He turned to the drug chart and started writing up pre-meds.

He had a patient to operate on. Medicine.

He needed to concentrate on practicalities, not emotion.

How many appendectomies had he performed in his working life? Max had lost count. He should be able to do this in his sleep, and yet enough had presented challenges over the years for his adrenaline levels to rise as he stepped into the theatre.

This place didn't have back-up, either. It had no highly equipped intensive care unit and no specially trained theatre staff.

It shouldn't matter. He'd already figured that Sam Taylor was extremely competent. A fly in, fly out surgeon and anaesthetist came once a month, but in the interim Sam and Keanu did most of the low-key surgery, even though they weren't specifically surgically or anaesthetically trained. Sam surely knew what he was doing now. He discussed the levels of anaesthesia with a calmness that spoke of years of practice.

And Hettie was good, too. She worked silently in the

background, not ready to pick up doctors as they collapsed, as Tomas had suggested, but surely ensuring nothing would collapse on her watch.

As Tomas slipped into drugged oblivion Max checked and rechecked the monitors, and got the go-ahead from Sam—'All systems go!'

And from Hettie came a curt, 'Yeah, why are you asking me?'

He made a neat incision—and almost immediately suspected something was wrong.

The appendix was gangrenous.

'No wonder he was hurting,' he muttered, and then concentrated a bit more and the mood in Theatre became tense around him.

Hettie and Sam had assisted in enough surgical procedures to know when things weren't great. There'd been the odd comment, a joke from Sam as Max had made the incision, and now there was silence.

'Blast,' Max muttered, and the silence intensified.

He closed his eyes for a nanosecond and then stepped back from the table. Hettie moved in with swabs.

'I need to change the incision to midline,' he told Sam. 'I'm thinking caecal carcinoma. That's what it looks like.'

'Can you cope with that here?' Hettie asked. It was a dismayed whisper.

Max was looking at Sam. 'It's extensive—I'm thinking a right hemicolectomy. Couple of hours, mate. You up for it?'

'We can't close him up and send him to Cairns?' Sam asked, and Max shook his head.

'Worst case—if we have to—but the mess of the gangrenous appendix is going to knock him around anyway. There's no way I can close and leave it. To close and send him for further surgery... The outcome's shaky anyway.'

'Okay,' Sam said grimly. 'What are we waiting for?'

And as if on cue the door to Theatre swung open. Caroline stood there, in her nurse's uniform, looking...scared.

'Dad?'

'Problem?' Max was checking the equipment tray with Hettie, figuring what else they needed on hand before he did the midline. 'We'll be a while, Caro.'

'That's just it,' Caro said, and he thought, *Uh-oh, she's scared.* 'We need a doctor out here. Billy Tarla's just come off his boat. He was dropping lobster pots on the reef and the rope wound round his leg. He fell and the pot pulled him under. His mate got him out but he was five minutes underwater. They've got him breathing but he's still unconscious. The boat landed five minutes ago. They should be arriving now.' She paused and listened and they could hear a car being revved up the hill, engine screaming. 'That'll be him. Dad, Sam...'

'Where's Keanu?' Max snapped.

'On one of the outer islands. Clinic.'

'Damn.' Two doctors. Two patients. Two situations ideally calling for two doctors each.

'Close and wait?' Sam asked, and Max looked down at the incision he'd already made and swore. The appendix was a mess. The longer he took, the more likely it would be that infection would spread through Tomas's body.

'If it's important... If I have to,' Hettie ventured. 'If you give me instructions every step of the way...I've given anaesthetics before.'

And Sam's face cleared. 'She has. She's good, Max.'

'Good enough to give an anaesthetic?' he demanded.

'I know it's unusual but we've used her before. She follows instructions to the letter. I trust her.'

And he knew Hettie well enough by now not to argue. Moving on... If Sam left... If Hettie took over the anaesthetic...

'I'll still need an assistant.' He wasn't being precious.

To do the complex surgery he was proposing and have to turn constantly to locate the equipment he needed was impossible.

'How about I stay?' Caroline suggested.

'Sam'll need the best help possible,' Hettie said. 'Send in Beth. She's not theatre trained but—'

'What's her training?' Max demanded, and Hettie gave a strained smile.

'Registered nurse, basic qualifications. She's only just returned from the mainland after qualifying. So no theatre experience yet but she's calm and she doesn't faint. You talk me through the anaesthesia, I'll talk Beth through what she needs to be doing.'

Outside the truck had screeched to a halt. 'Okay, Max?' Hettie said. 'Caro, Sam, go. Billy's Tomas's mate's son. If we give up on his life to save Tomas, Tomas will never forgive us. Let's give it our best shot and save them both.'

Hettie was, quite simply, incredible.

The surgery he was performing was complex, technically difficult and messy. Normally there'd be a team of at least four highly qualified medics. Beth was a scared newly qualified with just basic training. She was totally reliant on Hettie's directions. The thing was, though, that Hettie gave directions softly and succinctly, and so subtly that Max found himself snapping a request for something and it was in his hand almost before he needed it. Hettie was watching Tomas's breathing, watching the monitors, watching Max's hands, as if she had six hands and six eyes. And she wasn't even a doctor!

Occasionally she'd slip the odd query his way—or a warning as blood pressure dropped—and once she hit the intercom with her elbow. A scared kitchen lad came to the door and she requested plasma. He returned before Max needed it.

She was amazing.

He couldn't pay her any attention. If Tomas was to end up with a working bowel, Max needed to use all the skill at his disposal, and he could only be grateful that Hettie's skills seemed to match his.

Grateful? 'Astounded' was the word he wanted, he thought as he finally stepped back from the sutured and dressed wound and moved to help Hettie reverse the anaesthetic. He saw the sag of her shoulders as he took control; he knew how much stress she'd been under.

This woman must have spent her entire working life learning 'more', he thought. She must have watched and watched, and learned and learned, and he thought that for Tomas's sake, the day she'd decided to move to Wildfire had been a blessing.

'Thank you both,' he said simply, as Hettie started to help Beth clear up. 'You're two amazing women.'

'You're not so bad yourself,' Hettie murmured, but her voice shook and he thought she could hardly talk. Her concentration had been so fierce…

'We all did good,' Beth said in satisfaction, and then looked down at Tomas's drawn face. 'Will he…? Is he…?'

'He'll need chemotherapy,' he told her. 'But it's looking good. I'm pretty sure I've removed everything. He'll need to go to the mainland for scans and to see an oncologist. It's unfortunate but it's a small sacrifice when he's looking at years of life ahead of him. The appendix was a bit of a blessing. If it hadn't flared, the tumour could have grumbled and spread for a long time without us knowing. As it is, we've caught it early. Also, Sam ran blood tests yesterday and there's no sign of anaemia. Lack of anaemia in caecal carcinoma is related to a better outcome. If I was a betting man I'd say he has a few good years left.'

'Oh, thank goodness,' Beth said, and burst into tears.

* * *

No man is an island... Nowhere was that so true as on Wild-fire. Tomas was Beth's uncle. Hettie had known that when she'd asked her to assist. It hadn't been fair but there hadn't seemed a choice and Beth had handled herself brilliantly. Now it was over, it was fine to burst into tears—and Max had said exactly the right thing.

He hadn't treated Beth as a junior helping out, Hettie thought. His response to her had been as one medic to another. He hadn't patronised or sympathised and Beth had taken his words and held them. They'd be repeated to Tomas's wife, his mother, his children, and the reassurance would be all the better coming from Beth.

And by adding the comment about going to the mainland for chemotherapy... By the time Tomas was fit enough to put up a fight the family would have plans in place.

It's a small sacrifice when he's looking at years of life ahead of him.

That line would be repeated across the island, and Tomas wouldn't have a leg to stand on.

Max had saved Tomas's life today, Hettie thought, and he'd save it into the future.

So why did her knees suddenly feel like jelly?

'Sit,' Max said, and her gaze jerked up to his in surprise. *What...?*

'Sit,' he said again, more gently, and suddenly his hands were on her shoulders and he was propelling her into a chair at the side of the room. It was a chair put there for just such a purpose, only she'd never used such a chair in her life. But she was sitting and Max was easing her head down between her knees with gentle, inexorable pressure.

'Watch Tomas,' he growled to Beth. 'Tell me the minute his breathing changes. The second.'

'Go back to him,' Hettie muttered. 'I can manage.'

'I know you can,' he said softly. 'You can and you can

and you can. You're amazing, Henrietta de Lacey. I wonder if this whole island knows how wonderful you are.'

'She needs to be even more wonderful now,' Beth interjected. The nurse was bent two inches from Tomas's nose, watching his breathing with total attention, following Max's instructions to the letter.

'What—' Max started.

'The Child Welfare people.' Beth pointed to the clock. 'They'll be here in thirty minutes.'

'I need to check on Billy,' Hettie murmured. 'Sam and Caroline might need help.'

'I'll check on Billy,' Max said firmly. 'You go and get yourself ready to be a mother.'

Billy looked like he'd make it. He had water on his lungs. He'd need intravenous antibiotics and careful watching for a couple of days but for a potentially lethal accident the outcome looked promising.

'He was under for almost five minutes,' Sam told Max. 'He's probably knocked off a neural pathway or two, and, to be honest, he didn't have all that many pathways to begin with. Not the sharpest knife in the block is our Billy, which explains why he was tossing out lobster pots without checking where the ropes were. But he's conscious, he knows what day it is and with luck he'll walk away with no consequences. And Tomas?'

'Hopefully the same.'

'Excellent,' Sam said. 'You sure you don't want to join us permanently, Dr Lockhart?'

'No,' he snapped, possibly with more force than necessary, and Sam looked at him quizzically.

'I've hit a nerve?'

'I've had responsibility since I was twenty. I wouldn't mind some freedom.'

'Right,' Sam said slowly. He glanced at his watch. 'You going to this meeting with Child Welfare?'

'I'll go for Hettie but he's not my responsibility.' Why did he feel the need to say that so forcefully? Sam was looking at him in mild astonishment.

'He is your brother's child,' Sam reminded him. 'Ian's name is on the birth certificate. It seemed even though Ian paid for Sefina's marriage, Sefina was still adamant that Joni was a Lockhart.'

'He was Ian's son, not mine.'

'Yes,' Sam said gently. 'But with Ian's name on his birth certificate, and you being next of kin to Ian, you're his closest relative. You get to choose.'

'I choose Hettie.'

'I meant choosing whether to keep him yourself,' Sam said. 'I've been on the phone to the mainland for a couple of hours, being grilled on the situation, and I can tell you that Hettie will need your support and more if she's to be allowed to adopt him. So why are you still here? Or does your lack of responsibility mean you're not even interested enough to attend?'

'There's no need—'

'To be blunt? Maybe there is,' Sam said. 'If you care about Hettie, you need to be there now.'

He'd always intended to be there. Joni was his last responsibility. This was the last of Ian's messes to be cleared up.

But because of the medical emergencies of the morning he was late. He walked into the meeting, he looked at Hettie's face and he knew things weren't going well.

Sam had volunteered his office for the meeting and two officials were seated behind Sam's desk. They had a chair apiece and had pulled in a folding chair for Hettie. She was sitting facing them. It had the effect of making Hettie seem younger, vulnerable, like a schoolkid in front of two headmasters.

The man and woman were both suited, formal. Hettie had changed in a rush. She was wearing a simple blue skirt and white blouse. Her hair was still tugged back as it had been in Theatre. She was wearing no make-up.

She looked scared.

'Good afternoon,' Max said, and formally introduced himself. 'I apologise for being late—we've had medical emergencies, which have also prevented Dr Taylor from being here. I believe those incidents have also meant Ms de Lacey is less prepared than she'd wish to be. However, we have saved two lives so I'm sure it was worth the inconvenience. Now, before we go any further, this seating arrangement seems inappropriate. Let's pull this desk back and get ourselves a couple more decent chairs. Ms de Lacey has had a stressful morning; we don't want to put her under more stress.'

There were harrumphs and sighs but he went ahead and reorganised the room. He'd learned early with patients that behind-the-desk consultations could push stress levels through the roof. Informality put everyone on an equal footing and Hettie needed that.

Hettie cast him a grateful glance as they all re-settled, but he saw her fingers clench as soon as the woman in the suit started talking again. It seemed they were well into the discussion.

'Dr Lockhart, please understand that we've done some intense research on Joni's situation in the last two days.' The woman addressed Max as if she'd already finished her discussion with Hettie. 'His mother is dead. His stepfather doesn't wish to have anything to do with him—indeed, he's making threats if the child stays on the island. We understand criminal charges are pending but we can't take that into consideration—our principal job is to keep Joni safe.

We've made some tentative enquires to his grandparents in Fiji but it seems they'd lost contact with their daughter and want nothing to do with her child. Dr Lockhart, you're Joni's uncle but Dr Taylor says you don't wish to take on the responsibility, either.'

Then her voice softened a little. She became the compassionate counsellor, still talking only to him. Ignoring Hettie.

'Dr Taylor told us your son died three weeks ago,' she murmured. 'If that's the case, we don't blame you for stepping back now. You have no wish to replace your son. No one would.'

You have no wish to replace your son.

The words felt like a kick to his gut, and Max felt himself freeze. He'd never thought of such a concept.

He felt ill.

But to his astonishment Hettie's hand came out and touched his. She flashed him a look that said she understood; that the woman's words were ridiculous.

'No one can replace Christopher,' Hettie said, to the room in general. 'We all know that. Joni and Christopher are two different people. "Replacement" is the wrong word, and to put Joni's care into the context of Max's grief is inappropriate.'

'I didn't mean...' The woman paused, disconcerted, looking towards her colleague for help.

'What Maria means,' the man said evenly, 'is that you don't want the child, Dr Lockhart, and that's understandable. Your grief aside, you are his next of kin. We've made tentative enquiries. You've raised two children already. You seem admirably responsible so of course you could have custody if you want him. But you don't, so we need to make other arrangements. Ms de Lacey here has kindly offered—'

'There's no *kindly* about it. I *want* Joni,' Hettie said, and maybe only Max heard the faint tremble in her voice. Her hand was still touching his. Was she taking reassurance now instead of giving it?

'Very well,' the man said. 'Ms de Lacy has expressed a desire to keep him, but we fail to see it as an appropriate option.'

'Well, I do,' Max said firmly, and he found himself holding Hettie's hand. Staring down this officious pair together. 'Hettie's competent, caring and loving, and she has the backing of the entire hospital staff. She also has my backing. As Joni's uncle, do I have a right to ask that Joni stay in her care?'

'Frankly, no,' the woman said, collecting herself and moving on. 'As next of kin, if you want him yourself it's a different matter, but you have no right to delegate. Ms de Lacy, we've talked to the island doctors and to some of the island elders. It seems there's reluctance to accept the child among the islanders. As well as that, Ms de Lacey, you've never expressed a wish to adopt a child before. You knew Joni's mother only in a professional capacity. You certainly didn't know her well enough to prevent her suiciding—'

'That's unfair,' Max snapped, beginning to seriously dislike this woman. But the woman shook her head and continued.

'Ms de Lacey was occupied with her professional duties while Mrs Dason was distressed. We understand that, but we also understand that she'd still be occupied with professional duties if we allow her to try and raise Joni. She has no means of financial support apart from her career. Also, Ms de Lacey, if we allowed you to adopt Joni, he'll be staying on an island where the local community consider him an outsider. That disadvantage might be mitigated if he were to have the support of two loving parents, but our feeling is that you alone have little chance of providing sufficient support. We therefore think it's best for the child if he leaves the island and starts life in a new community with two parents. We're sorry, Ms de Lacey, but Joni will be returning to the mainland with us. Tonight.'

Silence.

Other women might have sobbed, Max thought. Other women might have reacted with anger. Hettie simply sat staring at the woman who'd made the pronouncement.

The silence lengthened. Max tried to think of something to say, and couldn't. Her hand still lay in his. He found himself gripping tighter. Was he feeding her reassurance—or taking it himself?

Or was it something other than reassurance? Guilt?

Or more. She was hurting and he couldn't bear it. And the vision of Joni was all around him, too, a little boy who was partly a Lockhart, his parents' grandchild, a toddler in his cot, keeping quiet because he'd been hit...

Hettie had had the courage to do something about it. Why didn't he?

And the thought he'd had the previous night suddenly was there, front and centre. Family...

Could he?

'Is there any way I can appeal?' Hettie asked at last in a small voice, and the woman gave her a sympathetic smile.

'My dear, you're not family. From all reports you're hardly even a friend. You have no support for the child among the islanders, and you have no family support yourself. What do you possibly have to offer Joni?'

'Love?' Hettie said in a bleak voice, in a voice that said it was already hopeless. And then she seemed to pull herself together. She tugged her hand from Max's and she made one last try.

'What if I leave the island?' she said. 'I can get a job in Cairns. That takes away one of your objections.'

What? Max thought. For the island to lose Hettie...

But it seemed that also wasn't an option. 'The islanders' antagonism is only one of many objections,' the woman said, more firmly now. 'This seems a spur-of-the-moment offer and we can't decide a child's future on such a whim. The issue is settled.'

More silence. Hettie stared down at the floor, her face blank. She looked...stoic, Max thought. She'd accept it and she'd move on.

But why should she?

What had the woman called this? A spur-of-the-moment offer? It was no such thing, Max thought. What Hettie was offering—had, in fact, given—was something as old as time itself. It was love. He'd watched Hettie when she'd realised Sefina was dead and he'd seen the grief—and the love. He'd seen her at the simple burial service for Sefina. Hettie had looked stoic then. She'd loved and she'd lost.

Hettie had offered to move to Cairns. The woman had called it a spur-of-the-moment offer. It hadn't worked.

Love...

The situation was a muddle, a chaotic tangle in his head. He was trying to get it clear, but, no matter how tangled, one thing stood out.

For whatever reason, however unlikely, Hettie loved Joni. And wasn't love the most important thing?

And as he looked at Hettie he felt something deep within his gut, something that hadn't stirred for years.

Love?

No. He didn't understand it. It was too soon, too fast, too crazy. He had to get himself together. He had to get this on a solid, unemotional footing.

He had to say the only sensible thing there was to say.

'I have a proposition,' he said into the silence.

Behind him the door swung open. Sam had promised to try and attend to back Hettie up, and here he was. He opened the door but then he paused, as if he knew how momentous were the words Max was about to say.

'I've told you,' the woman snapped, her professional smile slipping. 'You can't delegate responsibility.'

'No, but I can share,' Max said, and he thought, *What am I doing? I want no responsibility.*

But surely this wasn't taking it. This was simply handing it over in another way.

'How?' the woman snapped, and Max turned to Hettie and took her hand and smiled at her.

'Easy,' he said. 'Hettie de Lacey, will you marry me?'

Up until now this discussion had been loaded with silences. None had been as long as this one. It stretched seemingly all the way to the horizon and back, and then zoomed off into the distance again.

The woman was the first to recover. 'Is this some kind of joke?' she snapped, but Max didn't take his eyes from Hettie.

'I'd get down on one knee if I didn't have coral grazes all over both of them,' he said. 'But, Hettie, I'm serious.'

She didn't look like she thought he was serious. She looked like she thought he'd lost his mind.

'What...? Max, for heaven's sake...'

'Think about it,' he said, urgently now because he could feel the rising anger of the two officials behind him. 'Hettie, can we go outside for a moment?'

'Say what you need to say here,' the woman snapped angrily. 'We'll not condone any arrangement made purely—'

'For the good of Joni?' Max finished for her. 'Isn't this what the entire meeting is about?' Still he watched Hettie. 'Hettie, think about it. I believe I'm Joni's lawful guardian. I'm his closest kin. As Louis has refused any responsibility, any court in Australia will give me first right of custody, especially as I know what parenthood entails. I know what I'm taking on.'

'You don't intend to take it on,' the woman snapped, and finally Max turned back to her.

'In times of stress families need time to adjust,' he said. 'You know that. I've changed my mind, and that's understandable in the circumstances. The responsibility's mine, and I'll take it on as long as I have a wife to support me. If Hettie agrees to marry me, we'll take Joni for our own.'

'But...you don't even want to stay on the island,' Hettie whispered, and Max turned to her again, his gaze meeting and holding hers. His gaze was an urgent message— *Hush*, he was saying without speaking. *Don't argue. Go along with this.*

'I will need to come and go,' he agreed. 'But half the workers on these islands seem to work on a fly in, fly out basis. I will support you, Hettie, and I'll support Joni. I swear.'

'You can't...' Hettie whispered.

'Why can't I?'

'This is ridiculous,' the woman snapped, and Max shook his head, determined not to look at her again.

'It's not ridiculous. Hettie and I share a very deep friendship. She's been in my employ for many years now.' There was no need to mention it wasn't totally his employ—the hospital was part funded by the Australian Government and he hadn't actually met Hettie until this week. That was irrelevant.

'Hettie's one of the best nurses I've ever met,' he continued. 'She's competent, she's caring, she's wonderful. She also swims like a champion and when she kisses me she knocks my socks off. Hettie and I have both been married before. Up until now we've been looking at life through sensible, pragmatic glasses, but suddenly I'm thinking, Why not? Why not, Hettie, love?'

To say Hettie looked astounded was an understatement. She looked like she'd just been slapped on the face with a wet fish. It couldn't matter. There was nothing he could do to make this proposal more romantic. Or sensible.

He wanted to whisk her outside and talk through practicalities, but there was no way he'd leave these officials time to reorganise their opposition. This was a rearguard attack. They'd been left floundering—it was just a shame that Hettie had, too.

'Well, about time.' It was Sam, coming to Hettie's rescue. Coming to both their rescues. He stooped to kiss Hettie, as if the thing was already decided and she'd said yes. 'You two have been smelling of April and May forever.' He grinned across at the officials. 'The whole island's been wondering…I had a text from one of my more impudent twelve-year-old patients when I flew in yesterday morning,' he told them. 'Bobby "borrowed" his dad's phone to take a picture of the big fish he was planning to catch. Instead, he spotted our Hettie and Max at one of the most beautiful of the island's waterholes. He sent me the photo in twelve-year-old indignation, and asked should Nurse Hettie be allowed to do "yucky stuff"?'

His grin broadened as he flicked open his cellphone and held it up. And there were Max and Hettie after their morning swim yesterday. Or rather there was Max—you could scarcely see Hettie but there was no denying she was under there.

It had been quite some kiss. All the emotion in the world was in that kiss.

Hettie opened her mouth to say something but nothing came out. Actually, Max was fighting for anything to say, as well. Hettie's normal tan had turned to bright crimson. She looked like she was blushing from the toes up.

This was one kiss recorded for the world to see. It was one kiss that meant these officials just might see their relationship as real.

It was one kiss that didn't mean anything?

'So we have Joni's uncle and Joni's mother's friend,' Sam said, smiling from Hettie to Max and back again. 'Two people who risked their lives trying to save Sefina and who saved Joni. Two people who love Joni and who wish to marry.'

'But Dr Lockhart doesn't want the child,' the woman managed.

'I didn't see how I could love him,' Max told her, deciding he should stop looking at Hettie. He'd sprung this on her with no warning. It wasn't fair, but then, he hadn't planned this. He just had to go with it. 'But if Hettie's willing to share,' he continued, 'then I think we can provide Joni with a safe and loving home. Hettie? This is much earlier than I'd like. I know it's rushed but suddenly it seems the only sensible option.'

He turned fully to her then and took her hands in his. He held them, firmly, and waited until she looked up at him. His gaze held hers. *Trust me,* he was saying in his head, but the words he said out loud were different.

'Hettie, we can be a family,' he said. 'We can make a home for Joni.'

'And no one will ever give Joni grief about his background when he's our Hettie and our Doc Lockhart's son,' Sam said triumphantly.

'Sam?' Max was still focussed on Hettie.

'Yes?' Sam was practically bouncing.

'Shut up,' Max growled. 'It's time for Hettie to speak. Hettie, do you think…? Is it too soon to ask you to marry me?'

His eyes were doing all the talking. He'd thought previously that this woman seemed to be a kindred spirit. Could she guess what he was thinking now?

She looked at him for a long time. The lady from welfare made to say something but the guy beside her put his hand on her arm as if to restrain her. All attention was on Hettie.

'We can do this,' Max said softly. 'We can work this out. Together.'

And she got it. He saw the moment when she decided to trust him. He saw the moment she decided to put Joni's fate—and hers—in his hands.

'You really want to marry me?'

'I do.' How hard was that to say? To be honest, though, it didn't seem to be adding to his responsibility. In some way it seemed to lessen it.

'Yes,' he said. 'We can give Joni a home. We can make it work.'

'Okay, then,' she said, and he blinked.

'Okay?'

'Until I get a ring, okay is all you get,' she managed. 'Okay is fine until I see the diamond to match.'

And amazingly he saw the hint of laughter, the slight twitch of her lips. She was amazing, he thought. Stunning.

'When?' the woman snapped in a last-ditch attempt to gain control, and Sam looked from Hettie to Max and back again and obviously decided a little help was needed.

'The islanders don't have mandatory waiting periods like the mainland does,' he said, grinning broadly. 'I know,' he added as the woman made an involuntary protest. 'They'll need to satisfy the Australian legal requirements, but for now...I'm sure you won't object to an island marriage. This island is, after all, part of Joni's heritage, or it will be with these two as his parents. Now, is there anything else, or is Joni's future settled?'

The officials left soon after, without Joni, making angry noises about Max's indecision costing them time and money but with no arguments left. Sam needed to head back to the wards.

'But this is the best possible outcome,' he told them, shaking Max's hand and kissing Hettie. 'Brilliant. Max, we'll make an islander of you yet.' He left, still grinning, and they were left alone in Sam's office.

What had just happened? Max was feeling like he'd been hit by a truck, but Hettie looked like she'd been hit by a bigger truck. The wet-fish analogy was no longer big enough.

'You know this won't be a real marriage.' He said it too fast, wanting to wipe the look he didn't understand from her face. Was she feeling trapped? He hadn't meant that.

'I didn't...' She took a deep breath and tried again. 'I didn't think so. You're offering...'

'A marriage in name only.' Once again he'd said it too fast. 'I don't intend to stay on the island, but neither do I... did I...intend to marry again. I've had enough of responsibility to last a lifetime.'

'You will be responsible...for Joni. If you marry me...'

'I'm already responsible for Joni.' He said it more forcibly than he'd intended, but he seemed to have little control over his emotions right now. 'What I'm doing by marrying you is assuring his future.'

'By delegating the responsibility.' Her voice sounded as if it came from a long way away.

'I'll pay,' he said. 'Of course I'll cover the cost of his upbringing. And, Hettie, I will treat Joni as my son.'

'Even though you won't be here.'

'I'll visit. He'll be a Lockhart of Wildfire.'

There was a pause. 'How will Caroline feel about that?' she asked at last.

'I think she'll be pleased. She said if worst came to worst she and Keanu would take him.'

'But worst hasn't come to the worst,' Hettie whispered. 'Because you're marrying me to stop that. Max, I don't think I want to be married.'

'But we've both been married,' he said, cautiously now because there was no need to bulldoze her. If indeed she didn't want Joni enough to take this step, things had to be reassessed. 'We married with our hearts before. This is marriage made for practical reasons, sensible reasons. It's a marriage made with our heads.'

'But you kissed me.'

And there it was, the elephant in the room. The kiss...

'In retrospect,' he said cautiously, 'maybe that was a mistake.'

And, amazingly, a glint of laughter crossed her face again. It was an echo, a trace, and it was gone as fast as it had appeared, but it left him disconcerted.

'Meaning kissing could get in the way of a marriage of convenience?' she asked.

'It could,' he said, just as cautiously, and she nodded and fell silent again, and then she turned and looked out the window.

'Why?' she asked, without looking back at him.

'Why?'

'Why are you making this offer?'

He had to get this straight. 'Because I know how much you want Joni. Because I believe you'll make Joni a wonderful mother. Because it'll give you and Joni the respect you deserve on this island.' He took a deep breath. 'And because there's no one else I want to marry.'

She didn't turn back. 'What if...what if there's someone else I'd like to marry?'

'Is there?'

'Call me stupid,' she whispered. 'But I've always thought...one day I'd like to end up with someone who loves me. Darryn never did. My parents never did.' She shrugged. 'Sorry. Pipe dream. It's not going to happen. This is a fine offer, a wonderful offer. It's more than kind.'

'I don't believe I made the offer to be kind.'

'You did,' she said gently. 'And of course I knew as soon as you said it that the sensible thing was to accept.'

'You can still back out.'

'And lose Joni? No.'

'If you meet someone else… Hettie, there's always divorce.'

'You think I don't know that?' Still she was staring out the window, as if there was something out there that took her entire concentration. 'Max, you took my breath away—back there. I was prepared to lose him.'

'I wasn't prepared to let you lose him.'

She turned then to face him. Her face had lost its colour. She looked strained to breaking point. 'It'll have to seem… real,' she whispered. 'At least while you're on the island. I mean, if we marry in name only and never go near each other it'll get back to them soon enough. The authorities. For the first year at least…'

'The Lockhart house is huge,' he told her. 'Caroline doesn't want to live there after her marriage. You could move right in. It's big enough for us…'

'To be separate?'

'Yes.' And then he added, and afterwards he wasn't sure why, 'If that's what you want.'

'Why would I want anything different? But, Max…the big house? I'm staff.'

'You won't be staff. Of course you could still nurse if you want—but you'd be my wife.' And then he paused. The word seemed to echo.

My wife.

He'd had a wife once. It had been a disaster. He'd sworn…

'Things don't need to change,' she said—fast, as if she'd read his mind. 'Max, my villa is fine. I'm happy to stay there.'

'Your villa isn't my home. You said yourself the marriage needs to be seen to be real, and if Joni's to be a Lockhart he has the right to be raised in the big house.'

'But you don't want a wife there.'

'I'll get used to it.'

'You won't have to. You'll be coming and going.'

'Yes.'

'You really won't expect…'

'You to be a wife?' He tried to smile. 'I'm pretty good at cooking for myself these days. I iron a mean shirt. I've even been known to scrub a bathroom.'

'Wow, now we really are getting into the nitty-gritty of marriage proposals.'

'I do have a housekeeper, though,' he added. 'So we don't need to take turn about.'

'This is getting more and more romantic.'

'It is, isn't it?' he agreed, and then he grinned, suddenly relaxing. This'd be okay. He'd marry Hettie. Hettie would live in the big house and care for Joni. He'd stay here for a little longer than he'd intended, but he'd go back to work in Sydney. He'd fly in, fly out, maybe once a month to check things were okay.

They could live in separate wings of the house. He could still be independent. He could still be free.

But there were a few words that niggled, that Hettie had said, that couldn't be unsaid.

But I've always thought…one day I'd like to end up with someone who loves me.

She deserved that, he thought, and suddenly he was back at the pool, with Hettie in her crimson bikini, with Hettie melting into his arms.

He wouldn't mind—

'Don't even think about it,' she snapped, and he stepped back as if she'd slapped him.

'What?'

'If you're thinking about a little nookie on the side.'

'Nookie?'

'You know what I mean.' She glowered. 'This is complicated enough. No nookie.'

'Sheesh, Het, no sex? What sort of marriage is that?'

'A marriage of convenience. It'll be like the olden days. You're a Lord Wotsit with debts up to your ears and I'm a plain little heiress with warts and a crooked nose and millions you can use to restore your castle.'

'I can't see a crooked nose. But do you have warts?' he demanded, fascinated.

'Not that I'm admitting to.'

'You can show me. I'm a doctor.'

She choked then, laughter bubbling up again unbidden. But then it faded and her lovely green eyes grew serious. 'Max, if you indeed do this…it will be the kindest—'

'It won't be the kindest. It's self-interest,' he growled.

'Marriage with no nookie is not self-interest.'

'Providing my nephew with a woman like you for his mother is self-interest. You're brave, kind, funny… Not to mention skilled.'

'My head will explode. Cut it out.' Still her gaze was serious. 'Max, can we really do this?'

'I think we can.' He reached out and took her hands. He looked down at them for a long time. They were good hands, slim, tanned from years in the island sun, worn from years of nursing. Years of caring.

'I know we can,' he said, more surely now. 'This is sensible, Hettie. We can make this work. So when? Next week? We'll get Caroline married off and then do the deed ourselves.'

'No fuss,' she said anxiously, and he could only agree. He was having trouble getting his head around…everything.

'I need to find Caroline,' he managed. 'I need to tell my daughter I have a brand-new family.'

'A family of convenience.'

'I suspect you and I both know that's the only type to have.'

CHAPTER EIGHT

FOR THE NEXT few days Max hardly saw Hettie. Lawyers arrived from the mainland to help him sort out the mess Ian had left. He and Harry spent hours planning directions the island management could take. A new fly in, fly out nurse arrived and Hettie took leave from nursing. She took Joni back to her villa.

They weren't avoiding each other on purpose—were they?

Max couldn't think about it. After so many years of neglect, all his focus had to be on seeing his daughter wed. Arrangements between him and Hettie had to take second place.

Which suited him. He needed time to get his head around what was about to happen.

Caroline and Keanu had organised a wedding rehearsal and then a dinner for their closest friends the night before their wedding. Max dropped by Hettie's villa that morning and asked her to be there, but she refused.

'It's Caroline's time,' Hettie said firmly. 'She needs her dad to herself. She's had to share him often enough.'

Max had to agree. He went to the dinner alone but Caroline cornered him afterwards.

'What's going on, Dad? Are you marrying Hettie or not?'

'Not until after your wedding. Hettie and I both agree that comes first.'

'But Hettie's my friend and your fiancée. She should be here.'

That's what he'd thought but Hettie had been adamant. 'I don't need a social life,' she'd told him. 'Especially not now. Joni needs me. We need to bond.'

Hettie had been dressed in shorts and a T-shirt. She'd let her hair loose. She'd been hugging Joni. She'd stood in the doorway of her villa and she hadn't invited him inside, and he'd thought that was just as well.

After they were married they'd move to the big house and things would change. Or would they? He'd be leaving, heading back to Sydney, doing what came next.

'Dad, talk to me,' Caroline was saying. 'You are marrying Hettie?'

'You know I am.'

'Then she has to be included in tomorrow's ceremony. I thought the hope was that the islanders start looking on Joni as yours and Hettie's. You need to be a family for that to happen.'

'You're my family.'

'Yes, but now I have Keanu, and you have Hettie and Joni. You offered this marriage, Dad. You need to go through with it.'

How to tell his daughter that one part of him would love to 'go through with it'? One part of him thought Hettie was the most beautiful woman he'd ever met.

But the other part of him wanted—needed—to head back to the mainland and soak up the freedom he'd wanted for so long.

'You'll walk me down the aisle tomorrow,' Caroline said, and he forced his attention back to the here and now.

'Of course.' He smiled at his beautiful daughter. Caroline was showing no signs of nerves. She was glowing in anticipation of spending the rest of her life with the man she loved.

Was he jealous?

'I love it that you're here,' she said softly, and suddenly she reached out and hugged him. 'I know responsibility has always kept you in Sydney but I've always known you love me. I'm so glad the *Lillyana* didn't sink. I'm so glad you're free to start again.'

To start again... What did that mean?

'But you have to start,' Caroline continued. Since when had his little girl got bossy? She was certainly bossy now. 'Dad, tomorrow you'll walk me down the aisle, you'll give my hand to Keanu and then you'll sit in the front pew. And you'll sit with Hettie and Joni. I've chosen my new family. You've chosen yours.'

'Caro—'

'It's the way it is,' she said gently. 'We're both moving on, and isn't it wonderful?'

Max went round to Hettie's as soon as the dinner finished. It was late but there was still a light on in her front room. He knocked and she opened the door a notch and peered out.

The door was on a chain. That took him aback a bit. Most islanders didn't even bother to lock their doors.

'Hettie?'

'It's you.' She sounded relieved. She closed the door and fumbled with the chain and a moment later the door swung wide.

She was wearing pyjamas. Pale blue pyjamas adorned with pink flamingos. Her hair was tousled. Her feet were bare and she looked so desirable it was all he could do not to gather her up and claim her as his wife there and then.

Boundaries would have to be worked out, he thought. Boundaries were like fine gossamer threads—he had to look close to see them and they could be broken with one misstep. But they were important.

So he forced himself to stop looking at the woman before him and looked instead at the chain.

'Do you get nervous?' And then he looked more closely. The chain was shiny new, and there was a trace of sawdust on the doorknob. Like it had only just been put on.

'Is this about you and me?' he managed lightly. 'Are you scared I'll come to claim my own?'

'What, club me and drag me by the hair back to your lair?' She said it lightly but he could hear the trace of strain behind her words. 'Nope. It seems to me that I've agreed to go willingly to the big house—if that is indeed your lair.'

'It's the closest thing to a lair I can think of. You reckon I should put down a few bearskin rugs and hook mirrors to the ceiling?'

'And pop in a dungeon complete with shackles and whips. Um…maybe not.' She was smiling but still there was that strain.

'Hettie, what are you afraid of?'

'N-nothing.'

'You don't put chains on your doors for nothing. What's going on?'

'I…Louis was here,' she said.

'Sefina's husband?'

'Yes.' She bit her lip. 'Look, I'm overreacting. He was drunk. You know he bashed Sefina before she died? There's a warrant out for his arrest but Ky's the only policeman on Wildfire and he hasn't been able to find him.'

'But he was here?'

She tilted her chin, looking all at once brave, defiant and vulnerable. 'He was drunk,' she said. 'Well, that's nothing new. But it seems things have changed for him. He's a bully. He accepted Ian's money to marry Sefina but he bad-

mouthed her and he threatened everyone who even tentatively tried to befriend her. He threatened me.'

'When?' She was so small, he thought, but then he
thought she wasn't small. She was defiant even now. She
was five feet four of courage.

'When I reported her injuries to the police,' she said.
'When I told Louis he'd pay for what he was doing to her.
He said he'd hurt me and anyone else who tried to interfere
with...well, I won't tell you what he called Sefina.'

'That didn't worry you?'

'I told Ky.' She flinched and he saw her regroup. 'And
now Louis's in hiding but he's running out of places to hide.
He came to find me today, and he yelled at me. He says the
islanders are starting to blame him for Sefina's death. They
are, too. There are a lot of guilty consciences; a lot of people who looked the other way. Her death has made people
see the appalling place she was in. So Louis is getting a
hard time and no one's willing to support him. He says...
He said, "The kid should never have survived. If you keep
him the locals'll be rubbing my nose in it for the rest of my
life. Don't you dare try and keep him. You and the doc...
Bloody do-gooders. Get rid of the kid or I'll do it for you."'

There was silence at that, silence while Max assimilated
her fear; while he looked down at the chain she'd obviously
had installed in a hurry; while he looked at the defiance of
that tilted chin and saw the fear behind it.

'You told Ky this, too?'

'Yes. He's trying to find him. But word is that he's all
talk and he's gone back to Atangi. It was only the booze
talking. I should be okay. But Ky sent a guy to put on the
chain.'

'Wise but not wise enough,' Max growled. 'You'll stay
in the big house tonight. Both of you. We'll pack what you
need and you can come now. There's room.'

'Max, it's ten o'clock. I'm in my pyjamas.'

'And very cute they are, too. You can put on some slippers, or I'll carry you.'

She choked on that, laughter bubbling despite the seriousness of what she'd been saying. 'You couldn't.'

'Want to see me try?'

'Yeah, you might manage it if you sling me over your shoulder like a bag of potatoes, and I cling to Joni while you carry me. Not. Max, I've just got Joni to sleep. I can't move now.'

'But you would feel safer in the big house?'

'I… Yes,' she admitted. 'Bessie and Harold are there. With a housekeeper and gardener on site, Louis wouldn't dare come near.'

'And me.'

'And you,' she admitted with another attempt at a smile. 'Macho Max.'

'There's no need to be sarcastic.'

'Believe it or not, I'm not being sarcastic,' she told him. 'You are macho. I've watched you swim into danger to try and save Sefina. You did save Joni. I've also watched you perform as fine a piece of surgery it's ever been my privilege to watch, and now you're threatening to throw me over your shoulder in a fireman's hold. So, yes, macho.'

'So you will come.'

'No,' she said. She took a deep breath. 'Not because I'm being stubborn. Not because I have any sense of bravado. I know I'll have to live there when we're married. But not tonight, Max, when it's Caroline's last night in her home before she marries. Tell me the house isn't full of guests? It is, isn't it?'

'You could sleep in my room. I could sleep in the living room.'

'And have all your guests trip over you in the morning? Max, I'm not moving in until Caroline is well and truly married, until we can divide the place into sensible sleeping quarters, until we can start as we mean to go on.'

And she was right. The place was full.

He thought of Sefina. He'd seen the pictures Hettie had taken when she'd been admitted before the cyclone. She'd been thoroughly, brutally bashed.

Somewhere out there was the guy who'd done it. Somewhere out there was the guy who was threatening Hettie. Rumour said he'd gone back to Atangi. Rumour wasn't enough.

'I'll sleep here tonight, then.'

'You're kidding.' She shook her head. 'Max, you can't. Firstly, I only have one bed. Secondly, it's the night before Caro's wedding. She needs you.'

'Caroline is surrounded by bridesmaids,' he said. 'We've arranged to have breakfast together, alone. I can go home by then, after I've checked with Ky that he has someone to keep an eye on this place. I can kip on your sofa. Okay?'

'I… Okay,' she managed, and he realised that underneath it all she really was scared.

'And, Hettie, you are coming with me to the wedding tomorrow.'

'Caroline's already invited me. I thought I'd slip in…'

'You're slipping nowhere.'

'But—'

'You'll sit with Joni, in the front pew, as my future wife, as my family. You and Joni are under my protection and the sooner Louis understands that, the sooner the threat to you will fade. We're a united front, Hettie. That's what this marriage is all about.'

'Until you leave.'

'I'll keep returning. I'll keep you safe. You're my—'

'Responsibility,' she said flatly. 'I know.'

'I meant to say you're my family.'

'It's the same thing, isn't it?' she said, attempting lightness. 'I'm sorry, Max. I'll try to make your load as light as possible.'

'I didn't mean—'

'I don't want you to explain,' she said, and he heard the faint note of bitterness in her voice. 'I'm enormously grateful and I'm sure Joni will be, too. Okay, then. Let's go find you a blanket and a pillow. My sofa's not bad. Let's both of us see if we can get some sleep.'

As a surgeon on call, and as a father of a disabled son who had spent his life in and out of hospital, Max should have been used to sleeping wherever he found himself. He usually could.

Tonight he couldn't. He found himself staring up at the ceiling, listening to the bush turkeys scrabbling in the undergrowth outside the villa. It wasn't that he was nervous. In truth, he wouldn't mind if Louis appeared. He had Sergeant Ky's number on his phone. He'd spent time training in karate. He wouldn't mind a chance to face off with the guy who'd caused so much grief.

So it wasn't that that was keeping him awake. It was the fact that Hettie was sleeping right through that door.

She had Joni in with her. Soon after she'd left him to his sofa, he'd heard him stir. She'd heard Hettie rise and comfort him, crooning him back to sleep.

For years Max had cuddled Christopher to sleep. The sound of someone else doing it…

Someone else taking his responsibility?

Someone else doing the loving?

It was a strange sensation and it left him feeling unsettled. Especially as the one doing the loving was Hettie.

His wife-to-be.

Wife. The word kept echoing in his head. She wasn't his wife yet, but she would be.

She was so different from Ellie. Ellie had been young,

vibrant, carefree. She'd been full of the promise of life to come.

Hettie was sensible, practical, bruised by life.

Which was why this would be a sensible, practical marriage.

She'd be taking on Joni. He wouldn't have to feel responsible.

Why did he suddenly want to feel responsible?

There was a crazy thought. It wouldn't go away, though, and at four in the morning, when Hettie padded through the lounge in her bare feet to heat a bottle, he was still wide awake.

He watched her from the shadows as she quietly heated Joni's milk, and when the bottle was ready he spoke.

'Bring him out here,' he said softly.

She jumped almost a foot. She yelped.

'Yikes,' she managed when she came down to earth. 'Don't do that. I forgot you were there.'

So much for the vague thought—hope?—that she might be lying in the dark, thinking about him.

'Sorry,' he told her. 'I just thought…maybe Joni should start seeing me as part of the furniture.'

'Because?'

'Because I will be,' he growled. 'Hettie, I will keep coming back. He should see me as…'

'His father? He's never had one.'

'I don't—'

'How about he calls you Papa?' Hettie suggested. 'That's a nice encompassing word that could be Dad or could be Papa.'

'And you'll be Nana?'

'That's the Fijian word for mother,' Hettie said softly. 'I can't replace Sefina. I have no wish to try.'

'But you could be Mama.'

'I guess…'

'At least Mama doesn't sound like Grandpa,' he growled, and she chuckled.

'That's settled, then…Papa. He's waiting.'

'Bring him out. Unless you think it'd distress him.'

'No,' she said softly, slowly, as if thinking it through. 'He's got so much to get used to but he needs to get to know his papa.'

Which explained why two minutes later Hettie was perched on the sofa, watching him feed Joni.

She'd simply walked out and handed him over. 'Papa is going to give you your bottle,' she told Joni, and she sat right down beside Max, easing the little boy onto Max's knee. They were right beside each other. Feeding their… son?

Together.

And for some unknown reason it evoked sensations so strong it almost blew him away.

He'd never done this.

Oh, he'd fed children, all right, mostly Christopher. He remembered hours, days, weeks in the nursery for premature babies, and then in a succession of hospitals. Feeding his son. Watching nurses feeding his son.

In the times when his mother had brought Caroline to the mainland, she'd leave her to him to feed so they could 'bond'—but Caroline had hardly known him. Feeding her had been fraught, tense, with Caroline making it very clear she preferred her beloved grandma.

But now… Joni didn't know him. Joni hardly knew Hettie. Yet somehow he was lying cradled in Max's arms, sucking fiercely at his bottle, casting an occasional glance at Hettie as if to make sure she was going nowhere but then looking up at Max again.

It was like he was learning Max's face.

'He's learning to know you, Papa,' Hettie whispered, and Max managed a grin.

'Don't you start using it. I can see it now. One marriage ceremony with a difference. Will you, Mama de Lacey, take you, Papa Lockhart…?'

She chuckled, a lovely low chuckle that lit the night. That even had Joni looking up in wonderment and his eyes lighting with something that might even be a smile—if he wasn't concentrating so fiercely on his bottle.

'You want me to call you Max?' Hettie asked.

'Of course.'

'You mean you want it to be personal?'

There was a question. It hung between them while Joni kept feeding, his sucking slowing as he grew sleepier. He shouldn't need a night bottle anymore, Max thought obliquely, but it was a comfort. A personal need.

Do you want it to be personal?

Was that what Hettie wanted? Support in more ways than one?

A proper marriage?

'Max, I didn't mean… With personal…I'm not asking for romance. I'm not one for hearts and flowers,' she said hurriedly.

'I didn't think you were.'

'But I'll not have a husband who calls me Mama.'

'And if anyone else on this island's seen you in your bikini and heard me call you Mama they'd think I was nuts.'

She chuckled again. 'So I'm not past it?'

'You're not past it at all,' he murmured. 'You're beautiful.'

'There's no need to get carried away.'

'I'm not carried away,' he said, and suddenly the laughter was gone from the room. 'Hettie, you are beautiful.'

'I'm thirty-five years old. I might have been beautiful a long time ago.'

'How long since you looked in the mirror? How long since you listened to your chuckle? How long since you saw your smile?'

'Max...don't.'

'I'm only speaking the truth.'

She sighed then and lifted the now sleeping Joni from Max's knee. She carried him into the bedroom. She had a nightlight on. He watched through the open door as she settled the little boy into the hospital cot she'd borrowed. She took her time settling him, crooning a little, making sure he was deeply asleep.

Then she straightened and he thought she'd close the door on him and return to bed. Instead, she came back to the doorway and stood and looked at him. It was a direct look that seemed to bore straight through him.

'Max, don't,' she said.

'Don't what?'

'Start something you have no intention of continuing.'

'Hey, I only said—'

'That I'm beautiful. I know. At least, I don't know that I'm beautiful, and you know what? I can't afford to think it. I put beautiful away a long time ago and it's staying away. We need to keep this impersonal. If we need to refer to ourselves as Papa and Mama...'

'In your dreams...'

'Max, that's all we can be to each other.'

'We can be friends.'

'Friends don't call each other beautiful.'

'Of course they do.'

'Friends don't kiss each other...as you kissed me,' she whispered and he had no answer.

'You want to be free,' she said, still whispering. She made no move to come forward out of the doorway. It was as if she was making sure she had an escape route. 'You'll leave after the marriage ceremony.'

'I'll come back.'

'As often as you need to. I know. You take your responsibilities seriously and I honour you for that. I'm not exactly
happy that Joni and I need to be your responsibility, but I'll
wear that. It's…anything else that I can't wear.'

'Like?'

'Like falling in love,' she said, and her whisper was so
low he could hardly hear it. 'Max, I can't do that. I can't
afford to. Not with a man who doesn't want to be here.'

'I don't want you to…'

'Fall in love? Of course you don't, and I won't, at least I
think I won't, unless you keep calling me beautiful. Unless
you keep cradling Joni and looking up at me as if you want
me to share how you're feeling. Unless you kiss me again.'
And then she hesitated but finally the rider…

'Unless you care.'

'I don't think…' he said, carefully, because in truth he
had no idea how to respond to this. 'I don't think I can
stop caring.'

'Care as my boss, then. Care as my acquaintance. You
can't care as my husband.'

'How can I not?'

'Stay separate,' she said. 'We've both been separate for
many years now. We're probably good at it.'

'I'm not.'

'But you don't want to love me. You don't want me to
love you.'

There was a long silence at that. A loaded silence.

Love.

He thought of the way he'd loved Ellie, fiercely, pas-
sionately, throwing all cares to the wind. What a disaster.

He thought of the pain of loving Caroline, knowing he
couldn't give her what she wanted, knowing he'd had to let
her go to keep her safe.

He thought of the agony of loving Christopher, of losing him little by little by little.

Did he want to love again? Could he?

It was too hard an ask, and Hettie saw it. She smiled, a tiny, rueful smile that was almost self-mocking.

'Don't, Max. Don't even think about going there. You've done an amazing thing for Joni and for me. All I'm saying is that we can't complicate things by going further. Yes, I'll call you Max. I won't call you Dr Lockhart because you'll be my husband but you'll be my husband in public only.'

'So you'll call me Dr Lockhart in private?'

'Are you kidding?' she said with sudden asperity, with the return of the Hettie with courage and humour. 'That would be just plain kinky. You know exactly what I mean, Max Lockhart. I have no need to explain further. Just cut it out with the beautiful. Now, if you don't mind, I'm going to bed.'

'But you will sit beside me at the wedding tomorrow.'

'Yes, because that's public.'

'Of course.' He didn't have a clue where to take this from here, and apparently neither did she, because she backed a few steps into her bedroom.

'Goodnight,' she managed, and closed the door behind her.

'Goodnight,' he repeated, but it was all he could do not to add a rider.

Goodnight, beautiful.

'Fall in love? Of course you don't, and I won't.'

That was what she'd said but she was wrong. She'd just uttered an out-and-out lie.

Hettie settled Joni into his cot and tried to settle herself but settling was impossible. She'd just watched a man who would be her husband feed a child who would be her son, and while she'd watched, she'd felt her world shift.

He was big and tender and kind. He'd held Joni as she knew he'd held his own son for years. She'd watched the expert way he'd held the bottle, his big hands cradling Joni, manoeuvring the bottle so Joni wasn't sucking air. She'd watched the way he'd constantly checked that all was right with the baby's world.

With her baby's world.

He was staying here to protect her.

He'd put his life on the line to try and save Sefina.

He held her heart in his hands.

And there it was, as simple and as complicated as that. It was crazy to say she'd fallen in love. It was far too soon, far too crazy, far too unthinkable.

But still…

He was lovely. He was in her living room.

He was to be her husband and if he wanted her…

It was totally, absolutely unthinkable but the sentence kept ringing in her head.

He held her heart in his hands.

CHAPTER NINE

HAPPY IS THE bride the sun shines on?

It wouldn't have made one speck of difference if it had been pouring, Max thought as he walked his daughter down the aisle. Caroline clung to his arm as if she needed his support, but he knew it wasn't true. She'd woken smiling and she hadn't stopped smiling since.

His beautiful daughter was marrying a man whose smile matched hers. Her Keanu was an islander, a doctor, a man of fierce intelligence and integrity, and Max couldn't have chosen a man he'd be more proud to call his son-in-law. Caroline didn't need his support.

No one did.

'Who giveth this woman…?'

'I do,' he said in a voice that was choked with emotion. He released his daughter's arm and stepped back to the pew reserved for him. The pew where Hettie sat, cradling Joni. At his insistence.

Hettie reached out and took his hand and he was grateful for it. The way his daughter looked… A man could dissolve into tears.

'Hold Joni,' Hettie said, and suddenly the sleeping Joni was on his knee. He had something…someone…to hold. To care for.

He didn't need him, he thought, but as the ceremony proceeded he was more than grateful for the baby's presence. And for Hettie's. She sat by him, pressed lightly against him as if there wasn't quite room in the pew, but of course there was, for this pew was reserved for the bride's family and there was only him.

The ceremony was over. Handel's Trumpet Voluntary sounded out through the little chapel, joyfully triumphant, across the headland and over the island beyond. Caroline was laughing and crying all at once. She was hugging her father and because he was holding Joni she was hugging the bemused little boy, as well. And then she took her husband's hand and somehow enveloped them all in a wedding hug—Caroline and Keanu, Max and Hettie and Joni.

'I have so much family,' she whispered through tears. 'I'm so happy. Dad, you need to go for it, as well. Love Hettie as much as I love Keanu.'

And then she was gone, in a mist of white lace, to envelop Keanu's aunts and uncles, his grandma, the staff of the hospital and anyone else who was brave enough to come into her orbit.

'You must be very proud.' The voice behind him made Max turn. It was Harry, holding the hand of a woman Max now knew as Sarah, the woman who'd acted as a fly in, fly out surgeon one week a month. Sarah enveloped Hettie in a hug. They turned to talk, and Max was left with Harry.

'Are you ready to leave?' Harry asked, smiling across at Caroline and Keanu. For all his distraction, though, Max knew this man to be an astute businessman. A billionaire with power. It behoved him to stop thinking about Caroline for a moment—and also stop thinking about the way Hettie had felt beside him in the chapel.

'You're wanting to take over responsibility?'

'In a word, yes. These islands… In a sense they've cured me,' Harry said. 'They've made me see there's life beyond my injury and it would be my privilege to give back. But you, Max, you've been injured, too, and you've been giving back for years. Forgive me but I've made some enquiries about your background. It seems you're a skilled surgeon working in the public sector but you've also honed your skills in cosmetic surgery. You're the go-to surgeon for Sydney's society darlings. Do you enjoy that?'

Did he enjoy it? After a day working in the public sector, operating as he had here, to turn to men and women who were paying to keep the years at bay... No, he hadn't enjoyed it.

'It's lucrative,' Harry said softly, watching his face. 'I, too, am a surgeon. I know the choices we make. I know the doctors who choose to work for money and those who don't. I know you, Max Lockhart, and I believe you're the latter. But my spies also tell me that every cent of your lucrative cosmetic practice has been channelled back to the Wildfire hospital. Max, we've already discussed this, but the money you contribute would be a drop in the ocean compared to my fortune. I've already said I would like to assist. It would be my very great privilege to endow the hospital in perpetuity. You no longer need to do cosmetic surgery. You can step back and let someone else take over. Will you accept?'

And with that Max felt the last great burden of responsibility lift from his shoulders. He thought of the CT scanner, blown in the power surge at the hospital, and of the usual mass of paperwork to try and get government help to repair it, or the scores of cosmetic surgical procedures he would have had to perform if government help wasn't forthcoming.

Would he accept? Here was freedom in a form he had never dreamed.

'Thank you,' he said simply. 'The whole island would be honoured to accept your help.'

And then he paused as a burst of delighted laughter

sprang from the crowd. The islanders were tossing armfuls of frangipani over the bride and groom. Some had landed in Joni's hair. The toddler had lifted a handful, stared in wonder and then tossed the petals towards Caroline.

And he crowed in delight.

It was the first time Max had seen the little boy laugh, and, by the look of it, Hettie hadn't seen him laugh, either. Max watched Hettie blink away tears. He watched her hug Joni and then stoop with him, gathering more flowers to toss again. She was wearing a soft blue dress—incredibly simple, elegant, right. She had a frangipani tucked behind her ear. She looked...happy.

A happy ending.

And for a brief moment he forgot about freedom and let himself think, *What if?*

What if he stayed?

What was he thinking? Abandoning his dream? Harry was right beside him, telling him his dream was real.

For years, from the time he'd been twenty years old and he'd stood in the premature nursery as the father of twins, he'd thought of freedom. And now it was being handed to him. His financial obligations had been lifted. Caroline was safely married. Joni? He had to take responsibility there, but Hettie had shouldered that, as well. He could easily support them, from a distance.

Louis had been a threat to Hettie but the news there was reassuring, as well. Sergeant Ky had arrested him late last night, drunk, outside Wildfire's only bar. With island sympathy for Louis completely gone, the bartender had rung Ky to tell him where he was. Louis had broken the bartender's jaw, he'd smashed furniture, he'd even lunged at Ky with a knife. He was currently on his way to the mainland, facing a lengthy jail term, and the consensus was that the islanders, both on Wildfire and Atangi, were pleased to see him go.

So that left Max free. Hettie was safe. Joni was cared

for. He could do whatever he wanted. He could work wherever he wanted.

He could lie on a beach in Hawaii and do nothing at all.

Suddenly Hettie was back beside him, linking her arm in his. But this was a plan they'd talked about before the ceremony. This whole family thing was a pretence, a plan to have Joni accepted by the islanders. It wasn't real.

'What are you two plotting?' she asked. Joni was still on the ground, happily sorting frangipani flowers. She smiled down at him and then smiled up at Max, a smile that took his breath away.

She was beautiful. This place was beautiful.

Freedom... He did want it—didn't he?

'Harry's making plans for the island,' he managed, and Hettie turned her smile on Harry.

'Good ones?'

'Excellent ones,' Harry told her. 'We'll make your hospital first class. I'm thinking we won't stop at repairing the cyclone damage. I'm thinking we need a new wing with the extra services we could offer. More full-time staff.' He eyed Max speculatively. 'You know, if you decide to stay, Wildfire needs a good surgeon.'

'Of course it does,' Hettie said stoutly, and her arm tightened in Max's. 'But don't you look to Dr Lockhart. Apart from a few fly in, fly out visits to check on his new family, our Max is free.'

And that should've made him feel amazing.

It did—didn't it?

Their own marriage took place three days later. It was a quiet ceremony. 'Max's son died so recently. There's no way we want a fuss,' Hettie told everyone, and their friends were disappointed but understanding. But they had enough people in attendance to make a public point.

Caroline and Keanu were there, smiling and smiling.

They were leaving the next day on an extended honeymoon but they'd stayed to see Max wed.

'Because even if this is only a marriage of convenience, I think it's lovely,' Caroline told Max before the ceremony, hugging him soundly. 'And if you can make it more…'

'Neither Hettie nor I want more.'

'Really?' Caroline looked across to where Keanu was talking to Hettie and her eyes reflected her love and her happiness. 'I can't think why not. Dad, why don't you go for it?'

'You know why not.'

'I do,' she said, softening and hugging him again. 'But, honestly, Dad, freedom's not all it's cut out to be. I understand what's driving you,' she said, as he tried to frame words to explain. 'I've figured it out but I don't have to like it. Off you go and see the big wide world but know always there are people who love you. Including, I suspect, your Hettie.'

'She's not my—'

'She would be,' Caroline said softly. 'Given half a chance. She has all the love in the world to give, your Hettie. Just say the word.'

'Caro…'

'I know. Not my business. But let's get you wed and see where things go from there.'

So here they were. *Getting wed…*

They didn't use the chapel. It didn't seem right to make time-honoured vows in the chapel when their vows were being made for convenience, not for love.

Instead they stood by the lagoon, in the place where he'd sat that first night with Hettie and Joni. Hettie was wearing the same blue dress she'd worn at Caroline's wedding. Caroline had made her a wreath of frangipanis and pinned it to her hair. Her curls were tumbling softly to her shoulders. She was bare-legged, wearing simple golden sandals.

She was devoid of all jewellery and as Max slipped the ring of gold on her finger he thought he'd never seen her look as lovely.

With this ring, I thee wed.

He'd made that vow before, as a carefree student, a boy who'd never imagined what responsibility that vow entailed.

Now he was making that same vow—without the responsibility?

It felt wrong.

'I will look after you,' he murmured, as she placed a matching ring on his finger and made the same vow, and she flashed him a look that might almost be anger.

'I don't need looking after,' she whispered. 'This island is my home and my family. Max, I love that you're doing this. I love your reasons, but I don't need your care. I'm not your responsibility, so if that's what you're thinking I'll take off this ring right now.'

'Really?'

'Really.'

'That would be the shortest marriage in the history of the universe.'

'I'm up for record breaking.' She was smiling, for the sake of their audience, he thought, but her voice was deadly serious. 'We're doing this for Joni. Don't you dare take me on, as well.'

'I want to take you on.'

'As my friend.' Her chin tilted. 'As your wife in name only. As someone you can leave and leave again. I'll not hold you down.'

He couldn't reply. Their tiny audience was watching, a little bemused. They were speaking in undertones, only to each other. What did brides and grooms generally say to each other in such circumstances?

'Go ahead or not?' Hettie whispered. Still her eyes were challenging.

And how could he not go ahead? Why would he not?

But he would take care of her, he thought. He just wished...

What? There was no time to decide.

The vows were made. They were man and wife. The island's celebrant beamed a blessing.

'You may now kiss the bride.'

Their friends were smiling and waiting. Caroline and Keanu, with Keanu cradling Joni. Harry and his Sarah. Sam and his Lia, just flown in from Brisbane, via Cairns. Bessie and Harold.

Couples who'd listened to the wedding vows and were remembering or looking forward to their own. He could see it in their eyes as they smiled and clapped and waited for him to kiss his bride.

As they waited for him to kiss Hettie.

And it felt...wrong? It felt dishonest, like some sort of travesty, that he'd make these vows to this woman, that he'd kiss her now and claim her as his wife and not mean it.

It was sensible. It was what they both wanted.

He needed to kiss his bride and move on.

He set his hands lightly on her shoulders and drew her to him.

He kissed his bride.

She should take this lightly. She'd deliberately pulled back during the ceremony and she'd deliberately added a prosaic reminder that this wedding was in name only.

So this kiss should be a brief, formal kiss, as this ceremony was supposed to be. And indeed for an instant that was all it was. Max's hands took her shoulders, she tilted her face to meet his and their lips brushed.

She should have pulled back fast. He should have released her. They should have turned to their audience, job done, formalities complete.

Except they didn't. They couldn't.

Because they were still kissing?

How did that happen? One moment there was a light brushing of lips against lips. The next moment the hold on her shoulders tightened. The brush of lips was repeated and then she found herself standing on tiptoe so the brush could be something more.

For it was something more. It was a whole lot more. Max was kissing her as if he meant it, as if this was no mock wedding. He was kissing her as if he wanted her.

Want...

It was such an alien sensation that she had no way of dealing with it. She was shocked into submission—but no. Submission? This was no such thing.

She was shocked into desire.

He was kissing her and she was giving as good as she got. Why not? she thought in the tiny amount of brain she had left for processing such thoughts. It's not every day a woman gets married.

It's not every day a woman marries a man like Max.

And with that thought came another, insidious, sweet, a siren song. What if this marriage was real?

What if Max wanted her?

It was a fleeting thought in the few sensuous moments as his mouth claimed hers, as warmth flooded her body, as his hands held her to him.

As she felt herself mould against him.

As she kissed him as she'd never dreamed she could ever kiss.

And as the kiss ended, as she surfaced to laughter and applause and Max smiling down at her, his hands on her shoulders, she thought, *My world has changed.*

She was married.

It was a marriage of convenience.

Yes, it was, she told herself. Her head knew that it was true. It was only her body telling her it was a lie.

Or maybe it was more. For somehow she knew, deep down, admit it or not, it was her heart that was telling her that for richer or poorer, in sickness and in health, for as long as they both should live, this man was her husband.

Her heart was saying, Marriage of convenience or not, from his moment, with this kiss, she was truly married.

Only, of course, it *was* just a marriage of convenience. They signed the register. They received laughing congratulations from their friends. They got through a sumptuous wedding feast that Caroline had organised and then their friends dispersed and they were left alone.

With Joni.

'Let Keanu and I take him for the night,' Caroline had begged, but Hettie wouldn't hear of it.

'He's only just starting to relax with me. And with Max. He needs to stay with us.'

Plus she needed the little boy, she thought as she walked up the steps into the palatial Lockhart mansion. She looked at all the photographs of Lockhart ancestors and felt the presence of her new husband behind her and thought, *What have I done?*

Joni was practically a shield. She hugged him tight, thinking this was for him. Joni's rightful place was here. Max had wanted her to move in here three days ago but when Ky had assured her there was no further threat from Louis she'd opted to stay in her villa.

'Only until our wedding,' Max had growled, and she'd agreed, but now there was no reason not to live here.

Except she wasn't a Lockhart. This wasn't her home. It'd be more suitable if she was here as Joni's nanny, she thought, and a bubble of laughter that was half fear rose within her.

She should be the hired help. She had no place here.

And the way she felt about Max… It scared her.

'This is your room,' Max told her. He'd led her across the grand entrance hall and along a short passage. He threw open double doors and she caught her breath in awe.

This room was amazing. This room was bliss.

For a start it was vast. It was also old. The worn, wooden floor was honey gold and faded by sun. The bed was an enormous four-poster, with soft white netting draped around it. There was a faded chintz sofa and armchairs, a small, elegant antique table, faded rugs, and wide French windows opening to the verandah and the lagoon beyond.

The room invited her in, welcomed her in a way nothing else could. A woman could sink into this room.

'Check the bathroom,' Max said, smiling, watching her face. He threw open a door and revealed an enormous tub on crocodile feet, a shower the width of the room and massive towel rails with lush, white towels. All still looking over the lagoon.

'And this is where Joni can sleep,' he told her. He opened another door and there was a perfect child's room, already decorated with pink wallpaper. With ponies and roses and tiny forget-me-nots.

'This was Caroline's. Maybe we should get rid of the pink.'

'I don't think Joni's noticing,' Hettie said. 'But we… Maybe I can do something later? Max, it's beautiful. But where do you sleep?'

'At the other end of the house. But I'm leaving next week so you'll have the whole house to yourself.'

'That's…fine,' she managed, and hugged Joni a bit tighter.

'Bessie and Harold will be here. Ky says Louis is no longer a threat.'

'You don't need to worry.' But she must have sounded strained because Max looked at her in concern.

'Hettie, I didn't resign from my job,' he told her. 'I took leave. I'm not sure what I'll be doing in the future but for now, my job at Sydney Central is waiting.'

'Of course it is.' She struggled to make her tone light. 'But you will come back?' Heck, she sounded needy. She could have slapped herself but the words were out and she couldn't get them back.

'Once a month,' he told her. 'I have it planned. If I stay at Sydney Central I'll do what most fly in, fly outers do. I'll work through a couple of weekends and then spend five or six days here once a month. That way I can catch up with Caroline and with you and Joni.'

That was the deal, she thought. This was the agreement going into their marriage. This arrangement had given the little boy to her, and more. It had given her the backing of the Lockhart name, this sumptuous place to live, and a live-in housekeeper and groundsman to help with Joni's care.

How could she possibly want more?

It was just that kiss.

Those kisses.

They were somehow imprinted on her heart. How Max could stand there and calmly talk about catching up with her once a month when he'd kissed her like that…

'What you're planning… That doesn't sound like free-dom to me,' she ventured. 'Max, this has been all about me. I wanted Joni and I have him. What do you want?'

'I have everything I need.'

'I didn't say need. I said want.'

'Want doesn't come into it.'

'So all that talk of freedom…'

'Leave it.'

It was a snap and she flinched. He saw it and swore. 'Hettie, I didn't mean—'

'It doesn't matter.' She cut him off. 'I'm tired. Max, I need to settle Joni and go to bed myself.'

'Of course.' But there was a strain between them that was almost tangible. He was standing back, apart. That's what he wanted, she thought. His body language was almost spelling it out.

Why did she want to weep?

Some wedding night, she thought bleakly, with the groom backing out of her room as fast as he could go, with her holding Joni like a shield.

They were alike. Two people with ghosts, with shadows so deep they'd never move past them.

But she was overthinking things. This, after all, was a business arrangement, a great outcome for all concerned. If she could just get the kisses out of her head... If she could just look at Max and see the patriarch of the island, the hospital's benefactor, a fine surgeon, her friend...

Not the man. Not the toe-curlingly sexy male her heart told her he was. Not a man who knew how to love and who could be loved in return.

Not a man with needs he couldn't admit to.

No. That was wishful thinking and she needed sensible thinking. And action.

'I don't need anything else,' she told him, striving to sound brisk and efficient. 'I know where the kitchen is if Joni needs a bottle and everything else can wait until morning. Thank you, Max. Thank you for everything and goodnight.'

'It's me who should be thanking you,' he said heavily. 'You're the one taking on the responsibility for Joni.'

'I'm not taking on responsibility for anything,' she snapped, suddenly angry. 'I'm choosing. They're very different things and I'm sorry you can't see it. Meanwhile, I don't need gratitude.'

'Hettie—'

'Goodnight, Max,' she said, as firmly as she could manage, and she turned away fast, and if it was to hide the sudden moisture welling behind her eyes, well, how stupid was that?

A woman had to be sensible. A sensible woman said goodnight to her brand-new husband and closed the door behind him.

And where was sleep after that?

Max didn't even try to go to bed. Instead, he wandered down to the lagoon where a few short hours ago he'd made the vows to love and to honour Hettie de Lacey for the rest of his life.

They'd been mock vows.

They hadn't felt like mock vows.

It didn't matter, though, he thought as he stared out over the still water. He'd always look out for her. He'd keep her safe and he'd keep his nephew safe.

He was responsible for them—and he didn't want to be responsible.

But neither did he want to walk away.

He could stay. He could pretend those vows were real. To love and to honour… Well, the honour was real at least.

Love? He'd known her a week.

She was a convenient answer to the problem of Joni.

Could he love Joni?

As he'd loved Christopher?

A few short weeks ago he'd stood by his son's grave and he'd felt his heart break. Simple as that.

He'd done the same when Ellie had died. He'd had no idea that grief was a physical thing, a crumbling from within, a physical reaction that had left him gutted, helpless, without an anchor. Drifting as the *Lillyanna* had drifted, buffeted by whatever wind, whatever tide took her.

That's what grief did to you. That's what love did to you.

He'd longed for freedom and now he had it. If anything happened to Caroline, yes, he'd be gutted again, but she had her Keanu to look out for her. He was free.

A man without responsibilities.

Why did it feel so empty?

He was still feeling grief; of course he was. With his son so recently gone…how could he think of making new connections?

Of filling the void.

Of replacing Christopher?

Hell.

It was hell. His head was filled with a special kind of torment, a tangle of pain and confusion and emptiness.

What he wanted—what he ached for—was to walk back into the house, take Hettie into his arms and hold her. To take comfort in her body. To forget himself in the love he suspected she could give.

She'd given her heart to Joni but he was starting to know this woman. He'd kissed her and she'd kissed him back, and there was a matching need in that kiss. The difference was that her need wasn't a product of aching loss.

What was it, then?

The beginnings of love?

If it was…

If it was then he had to move away fast. It wasn't fair on Hettie to take this one step further. He'd married her because it had been the sensible thing to do. To even think about making that marriage something other than a signed contract would be to invite disaster.

To let her hold him when he couldn't give back… To ask her to love him when all he felt was fear… It was unthinkable.

He swore and a night heron startled and flew straight upward into the starlit sky.

The night stretched on but still he didn't go inside. He

needed to go back to Sydney, he thought, and quickly. He needed to bury himself in his work. There was always enough medicine to fill the void. In Theatre, with lives under his hands, there was no room for the questions hammering in his head.

He could go back to swimming laps, lifting weights, running, filling the empty crevices of his life. He could finally figure where he could go from here without pain.

Except…why was the pain still with him?

It was Christopher, he told himself. Of course it was Christopher. He ached for his son.

He stood and looked out over the lagoon until the first rays of dawn tinged the sky.

He thought about Christopher. And Ellie.

It was sheer discipline that stopped him thinking about Hettie.

CHAPTER TEN

THE NEXT FEW DAYS were busy—deliberately so. He and Harry spent hours delving into the island's finances, deciding what needed to be invested and where. The knowledge that he wasn't on his own was incredible. Since his father's death he'd felt the full responsibility for the island's welfare. Now...the sensation of sharing made him feel almost light-headed.

'Harry's hiring choppers from the mainland within the next week,' he told Hettie on the night before he left. 'We've planned a full spray of all the M'Langi islands. Until now I've only been able to do Wildfire but if we can get rid of the mosquito breeding grounds... With the new vaccine available for clinical trials, with the money injected to get stocks, with the spray covering the swamp areas, encephalitis might become a thing of the past. And the ulcers... Without them, this island will be so much safer.'

He'd come back to the house—briefly. He'd done a couple of minor operations during the week and he'd told Sam he'd do a ward round that night.

'There's no need,' Sam had growled. 'Spend your last night with Hettie.'

But that was dangerous territory. He did need to be seen to spend time with her. That was part of the plan—to have the islanders see them as a family, to see Joni as a Lockhart—but that could easily be done with Hettie living in the house and Max dropping in and out at need. And sleeping—or not sleeping—there. Lying in the dark, thinking…

Trying not to think.

'You and Harry seem to have done a wonderful job,' Hettie was saying. She was sitting at the kitchen table. Joni was in his highchair. She was giving him his dinner, making the spoon into an aeroplane, making him giggle.

What was there in this scenario that made him want to run?

He didn't need to run. He was leaving tomorrow.

'Harry's amazing. I'm leaving the island in great hands.'

'But you still own the island,' Hettie said.

Was that a rebuke?

Maybe not. The aeroplane swooped, Joni chortled and the moment was past.

'You will be okay,' he told her.

'I'm not worrying about me,' she said, and then she stopped zooming the aeroplane and turned and looked directly at him. 'I'm worrying about you.'

What was there in that that took the air from his lungs?

'Why would you worry about me?'

'Going back to the mainland alone. Max, tell me you have good friends who'll meet you at the airport, who'll take you out to dinner, who'll watch your face and know you need to be taken for a drink or a walk or just have silent company. Christopher's so recently gone. Tell me you have friends who care.'

'My colleagues care.' They did, too, he thought. The hospital team had been incredibly supportive throughout Chris's illness. Some of his colleagues had attended the funeral. There'd been a vast arrangement of exotic flowers delivered to his apartment. His anaesthetist and a couple of his fellow surgeons had clapped him on the shoulder and said things like, 'We're with you, mate. Anything we can do, just ask.'

But he'd been so busy... For twenty-six years he'd been busy, working two jobs and caring for Christopher. He'd had an apartment at the hospital and a full-time carer for Chris, so that any gap in his working day could be spent with him.

Gaps hadn't included making friends.

Maybe he could now. Maybe that was what this new-found freedom would give him.

Friends.

He looked down at Hettie serenely feeding Joni, and he thought...

No. Run. Get out of here before the whole nightmare starts again. The nightmare of caring.

'I'm heading back to the hospital now,' he told her. 'I'll do a ward round tomorrow, too, before I go. I expect I'll see you at breakfast.'

She didn't move. 'I expect you will.'

'What will you do while I'm away?'

She concentrated on another aeroplane. 'Pretty much what I'm doing now, I expect. My role as charge nurse will be filled while I have some family leave.' She smiled up at him then. 'Actually, you know what? I intend to do...nothing. Or not quite nothing. I intend to play with Joni, to hug him, to take him to the beach and teach him to paddle, to lie under the palm trees and read silly kids' books to him. I intend to feed him his dinner via aeroplanes. I expect to leave my hair untied, wear my sarong, wake when Joni wakes, sleep when Joni sleeps. I intend to love my son.'

There was nothing to say to that. He glanced at Joni, who was picking up a rusk and inspecting it for possible poison. It was obviously a Very Suspicious Rusk, covered with Vegemite, the lovely black goop beloved by every true Australian kid but obviously not by Joni. He eyed it from every which way, then smeared it carefully onto his nose before carefully dropping it overboard.

Bugsy had been lying unnoticed in his basket by the corner. With the speed of light the rusk was hoovered up and Bugsy was back in his basket, smirking.

Joni chortled with delight and then looked expectantly at Hettie and held out his hand.

'Rusk?' he said, and Hettie giggled and Max grinned. But inside...his heart twisted.

'I have to go,' he said, and Hettie rose and searched his face.

'Do you?'

'You know I do.'

'I guess I do,' she said evenly, and then she took a deep breath. 'Max...I have to tell you, though...'

And then she fell silent.

Don't ask, he thought. *Just go*. But she was standing in front of him, shorts, T-shirt, snub nose, her curls a bit tangled. One curl had dared to drift across her eyes and she didn't seem to notice.

He really wanted to lift it and tuck it behind her ear.

He couldn't.

He should turn and walk out the door but his feet seemed glued to the floor.

'What?' he asked, heavily, and here it came.

'You should know that there's a choice,' she whispered. 'These last few days... I know you don't want it and I don't want you to take it any further. But what I feel for you... It's not gratitude. It's not respect and it's not friendship. You know how I held Joni after his mother died and I knew I could love him? Well, like it or not, that's how I feel with you.' She gave a wry grin then, as she heard what she'd said.

'Okay, sort of different,' she conceded. 'It's something to do with you being six feet tall and so gorgeous it's not fair to expect my hormones not to react.' She caught herself,

trying to make what she was saying make sense. 'Um...
Max...hormones or not, I understand you need to leave.
I respect that. I know your reasons. But when you come
back...I'll stay at my end of the house for as long as you
wish, for Joni's sake, but if you ever want me... If you ever
want to take it further...'

And then she broke away. She took a step back, looking appalled.

'Whoa, I'm sorry,' she managed. 'I can't imagine why
I'm laying this on you. I know it's not fair. But, Max, you
know I'm fine on my own. You know I'm happy. It's just
that I thought maybe if we're husband and wife I should
just say it. Just so you know...the hormone thing is sort
of...there.'

'I can't,' he said, because it was all he could think of to
say, and she nodded as if this was a normal conversation
between a married couple, maybe Mum asking Dad to take
the kid to school, Dad saying he couldn't.

Dad saying he couldn't commit.

Dad saying he couldn't be a dad. Or a husband.

Or a lover.

And there was the crux of everything. He wouldn't mind
being a lover. No, that was wrong. He *wanted* to be a lover.
The more time he spent with Hettie the more he wanted
to pick her up and carry her to his bed. To love, to protect,
to honour...

To hold her as his own.

But with that came the rest. Husband. Father. Island
patriarch. All the things that had weighed on him for
twenty-six years.

'Hettie, love...'

'I know I'm not your love.' She managed to say it
evenly, emotion gone from her voice. She sat down again
and started wiping Joni's face. 'I'm not your anything,' she
added mildly. 'I shouldn't have said it but it seemed only

honest and I think honesty has to be front and foremost in this…arrangement. Go back to work, Max. Go back to what you do and forget all about my dumb little confession. It means nothing. Your plane gets in at ten in the morning. I'll feed Joni between seven and eight but then we'll go and play by the lagoon. So if you can arrange not to be in the kitchen between seven and eight…'

'Why?'

'Because goodbye should be now,' she said, and she looked up at him and he saw the emotionless facade slip. He saw distress. 'Because I've just made a fool of myself and I need time to recover. You'll be back in a month and by then I'll have myself nicely under control. Joni and I will have our lives sorted. So you head off and sort your life as you want it to be—as you deserve it to be—and leave us to get on with ours.'

'Hettie—'

'Leave it, Max,' she said, and she tugged Joni from the highchair and held him close. 'I'm taking Joni for a bath so we'll say goodbye now.' And then she slipped forward and reached up and kissed him, lightly, a faint brush on the cheek. And then she stepped away fast.

'Goodbye, Max,' she whispered. 'And thank you.'

How was she to calmly bath Joni after that?

Luckily Joni pretty much bathed himself. He splashed in the big tub, crowing with delight as he ran water from a plastic mug down his tummy. He was entranced with his cleverness.

So was Hettie, but not completely. She sat on the floor next to the tub and she kept a hand on Joni's shoulders, keeping contact, keeping the reassurance that she was always there, and stupidly, foolishly, she let herself weep.

She'd just let down all her defences.

She was married and, for better or worse, she wanted

her husband. She wanted to keep contact. She wanted the reassurance that he was always there.

More, she wanted him.

At midnight, twelve-year-old Indi Hika and his two mates sneaked out of their parents' houses, took Indi's dad's dinghy and tried to catch flounder in the lagoon. Two hours later, hauling the dinghy out through the marshes, Indi felt a sting on his ankle. It hurt, but twelve-year-olds didn't make a fuss in front of their mates. By the time he limped home it was hurting a lot, but he was understandably reluctant to let his parents know he'd been out on the water after midnight. He sneaked back into bed and pulled up the covers.

He didn't even look at his ankle. If he had he would have seen two distinctive fang marks. Instead, he lay silent for two hours while his foot grew more and more painful and the venom spread through his body. Finally he cried out loud. His parents investigated, to find him twisting in agony and having trouble breathing.

The family had no phone. Max was standing on the house verandah, staring into the darkness, when he saw the truck race up the hill.

His thoughts were so tangled that a medical emergency was almost a relief. He reached the hospital almost as the Hikas did, and by the time Sam arrived he had the lad intubated.

It took the two doctors' combined efforts, considerable skill and the rest of the night to keep the boy breathing. Finally, though, Indi decided to live and Max walked out of the hospital to a new day. The day he was to leave.

He glanced at his watch. He had an hour until the plane left.

Hettie and Joni would have already breakfasted. She'd have taken him to the little beach at the end of the lagoon.

His time on the island was over.

He walked back to the house to shower and collect his gear. His thoughts were still drifting, the drama of the night fresh and real. Just do what comes next, he told himself as he walked up to the airstrip with his kitbag. Any number of people would have driven him but he wanted no one. He felt curiously disengaged, as if he was moving in a vacuum.

The *Lillyana* was in harbour, waiting for repairs. Most of his gear was still on her and could stay there.

His kitbag was light. He was…free.

It was the end of an era. He'd come back, he knew, but only as a visitor. The responsibilities had all been taken care of.

He'd be welcomed as a friend.

He wasn't part of this island.

The incoming plane hadn't arrived yet and the airstrip was deserted. He sat on a cyclone-smashed palm beside the hangar and looked out over the island. From here he could see the sea and the lagoons dotting the island. He could see across to the research station with the beautiful pool where he and Hettie had swum.

She'd keep swimming there.

And suddenly her words from the night before were replaying in his head. Not the ones concerning him. Not the ones that had him closing down, the words he didn't know what to do with. What he was remembering was her talking of taking family leave to get to know her new son.

'You know what?' she'd said. 'I intend to do…nothing. Or not quite nothing. I intend to play with Joni, to hug him, to take him to the beach and teach him to paddle, to lie under the palm trees and read silly kids' books to him. I intend to feed him his dinner via aeroplanes. I expect to leave my hair untied, wear my sarong, wake when Joni wakes, sleep when Joni sleeps. I intend to love my son.'

He found himself smiling at the thought of Hettie free

from her responsibilities as nurse manager, free to do what she wanted.

Free to love her son.

And all at once he was hit by a sensation so powerful he couldn't deal with it. It was like a blow to the side of the head, a blow that sent him reeling.

He wanted...what Hettie had chosen.

Of course he did, he told himself, rising and striding across to the edge of the clearing, staring across at the island and then out to the farther islands dotting the sea beyond. He wanted freedom. He'd ached for freedom. That's what Hettie now thought she had.

So...had he got it wrong?

Was freedom sitting under a palm tree, reading a kids' book to a child who wasn't his?

Was freedom dipping his toe again into the pool of loving?

Was freedom jumping right in?

The memories of the night just gone were still swirling in his head. Indi, twelve years old, agonisingly close to death. Indi's parents, clutching each other in terror, every fibre of their being centred on the life of their son. If he'd died, everything would have fallen apart.

As his life had fallen apart when Ellie had died. And then when Christopher had died.

He never wanted that pain again. If he walked away now, he'd never have it, and that was what he wanted—wasn't it?

'I intend to love my son.'

There was the rub. What if Joni were to be bitten by a snake or stand on a stonefish? Hettie would bear the trauma alone.

No, she wouldn't, he told himself savagely. She'd have every islander beside her. His own daughter and her husband would be here. Caroline and Keanu would support her. Everyone here would love her and stand by her.

It should be him.

He wanted it to be him.

He thought tangentially of Christopher. His grief for his son was still a raw and jagged wound. Surely he couldn't open his heart to that sort of loving again?

Surely he couldn't.

But as he stood in the morning sun, as he watched the silver glint of the incoming plane slowly grow bigger, he thought somehow, some way, he already had.

It wasn't a betrayal of Christopher. Or of Ellie.

He remembered Chris in one of the last few lucid moments before he'd slipped into unconsciousness. His lovely son had reached out and taken his hand.

'Dad, get a life...'

Chris had said it to him often, sometimes teasing, sometimes exasperated, a kid not able to see how seriously a man had to take the world.

Get a life.

A life could be...right here on the island.

Hettie was right here.

The choking fog that seemed to have enveloped him since Christopher's death was lifting, and with its lifting came a knowledge so deep, so fundamental that he must have been blind not to see it all along.

He was free to choose.

He could choose to love.

If she'd have him.

'Please,' he said out loud, and he left his kitbag where it lay and turned and started walking down towards the house. Towards his home.

And then he started to run.

Hettie and Joni and Bugsy had sat on the beach at the lagoon for a couple of hours. Joni was ready for a sleep but she hadn't wanted to risk running into Max by heading back to the house too soon. The plane's schedule was tight, though. It'd come in, drop off, pick up and be gone, so as soon as she saw it coming in the distance she knew it was safe to go home.

Home? To the Lockhart homestead.

She was a Lockhart. It'd take some getting used to. She was Max Lockhart's wife.

She was a wife without a husband.

She pushed the all-terrain stroller along the path to the house. The going was rough through the bushland, over leaf litter strewn from the cyclone. Joni was growing sleepier and she was in no hurry. What was the use of hurrying?

As she walked somehow she kept noticing the glint of gold on her ring finger.

She was married—and yet not.

She was married to a man who was even now boarding a plane to head back to Australia.

'Well, what did you expect?' she muttered to Bugsy, who was trailing at her side. 'He's given you Joni. What else did you want from him?'

'Nothing,' she told Bugsy.

She lied.

'Yeah, and didn't I do that well,' she demanded. 'Telling him I was available if he wanted me. Throwing myself at him. What sort of a goose must he take me for?'

Bugsy looked supremely disinterested. Joni, however, looked up sleepily from the stroller and looked a bit worried.

'It's okay, sweetheart,' she said, giving the stroller a final shove up the path into the clearing by the house. 'I'll forget to blush in a while. Life will settle down. We're fine on our own.'

But then Bugsy gave a joyful woof, as if he'd seen someone in the bushes. He lurched ahead. Hettie shoved the stroller up the last bit of rough path—and Max was in front of her. Max, looking dishevelled. Max, out of breath.

Max, looking as if he'd been running.

For a moment neither of them spoke. She couldn't, and it seemed neither could he. Possibly because he had no breath.

'Hey,' she whispered at last. 'You'll miss…you'll miss your plane. It's landed.'

He told her where the plane could go and she blinked. 'Pardon?'

'You heard. But I hope Joni didn't.' He smiled then, a tired, rueful smile. They were standing eight feet apart, as if he wasn't ready to venture closer. 'I guess…I need to start watching my language all over again. Toddlers are parrots.'

She hesitated, still confused. 'Joni's nearly asleep. I think you're safe. But…Max, I saw the plane coming in to land. That's why we're going home. Because you won't be there.'

There was a silence at that. It stretched on, while a couple of crazy parrots turned somersaults in the palms above her head, while a blue-winged butterfly idled past her nose, while she became aware of the look of strain behind Max's eyes.

'I guess,' Max said at last, as if he'd finally regained his breath and was ready to go on. 'What I'm about to ask… Hettie, do you think, in the future—or even now—do you think you can go home because I *am* there?'

She thought about it. Thinking was hard when there was a butterfly doing circles around her head, but it seemed it needed to be done. She needed to concentrate really hard.

She waved away the butterfly. The butterfly was beautiful but Max's words were better.

But this was a time to be practical, she told herself. She needed to say it like it was.

'Max, I'm truly grateful,' she managed. Why was it so hard to get her voice to work? 'I'm incredibly grateful for all you've done, but you've done enough. I won't have you staying because you feel responsible for me. For us. You need your freedom, and you deserve it. You need to leave.'

The silence stretched on. There were sunbeams filtering through the wind-battered canopy of palms. They were making odd shadows on the path. She concentrated on the patterns, on the shifting shadows.

Joni was drifting off to sleep in his stroller. He gave a tiny, sleepy murmur and Hettie checked him, grateful for the distraction. When she glanced up again Max's face had changed a little. The tension on his face lifted.

'Hettie, I know you don't need me,' he said, and it was as if he was talking from a long way away. This was a voice she hadn't heard before. 'But what if I realised...' he said slowly. 'What if I said I needed you? You take the world on your shoulders, Hettie, love. Could you take me on, too?'

What was he saying? She stared at him and then looked down at the shadows again. This felt terrifying. She felt as if she was on the edge of something so huge...

So fragile...

'Hettie, this might not make any sense to you,' he said slowly, as if he was still putting the words together in his head before he spoke. 'But I sat up on the runway, waiting for the plane to land, and I thought of you building sandcastles with our son—*our son*—and I had a wash of need so great it knocked sense into me.'

'Sense?' She was having so much trouble getting her voice to work.

'Perspective? Heaven knows what. I only know that at twenty I was landed with twins and financial obligations and responsibility and I coped. But you know what? Sometimes I even had fun. I loved Chris. I adored my daughter, even though I seldom saw her. But I loved it that Caroline grew to love this island, so much so that she's now married an islander. And I loved my work. Heaven help me, sometimes I even loved the weird and wonderful people who lined up to have themselves look younger. But all the while, all these years, a voice has been hammering in my head, saying, *What if you were free? What if you had none of these responsibilities?* And then suddenly...I was.'

'You deserve—'

'Who knows what I deserve?' he said frankly. 'But is what I deserve what I want?'

'I don't know what you mean.' It was barely a whisper.

'I mean I sat up there, waiting for the plane to take me to this new freedom, and I thought, Harry's taken financial responsibility from me. You've taken the care of Joni from me. Caroline and Keanu are here to take care of the island. I'm not needed. I can go and lie on a beach in Hawaii. I can do anything I want. And the plane was coming closer and I thought, I can get on that plane and go anywhere in the world. I'm needed nowhere. But then I thought, *Where do I want to be?* And suddenly the answer was so obvious it was like a punch to the side of the head. Because I knew. Hettie, I knew that you were at the lagoon, playing with our baby—*our* baby, Hettie—and I realised that this is where I want to be. More, this is where I need to be. Hettie, love, I'm not here because you need me. I'm here because I need you.'

The butterfly had landed on the leaf litter just beyond her feet. Its wings were still fluttering, seemingly in time with the beats of her heart.

She was trying to get Max's words into some sort of order. Some sort of sense.

For some reason, it was easier to watch the butterfly.

'This is probably way too soon,' Max said ruefully. 'I know you said you could love me but maybe you need time. Maybe we both need time.'

'Do you need time?' Her voice was still strangely calm.

'No,' he said, and he said it almost fiercely. 'I need no time at all. For I know what I want and I want you. Hettie, love, suddenly I have freedom and it's the greatest gift of all. Up on the airstrip as the plane was coming in to land… It was like a clearing of the fog. I could see it and why I couldn't see it before… But I am seeing it now. Hettie, it means I have the freedom to love. If you'll have me, my love. If you'll take me on, then I have the freedom to love you.' He paused, still apart from her, still holding himself back. 'But if it's too soon…if indeed we are rushing things… Hettie, tell me to go away and I will.'

'N-no.' It was so hard to make her voice work. 'Can you really want to stay?' she managed.

'For as long as you need me.' And then he shook his head. 'No. Let's make that as long as I need you.'

'And how long could that be?' Her voice was scarcely a whisper.

'Forever?'

Maybe she hadn't heard right, she thought. Maybe this was nothing but a dream.

But he was stepping forward. He was moving the stroller with the sleeping Joni aside and he was taking her hands. He was smiling at her, tenderly, lovingly but, oh, so uncertainly.

He thought she didn't need him.

Ha!

But let him think it, she decided, a hint of the inner Hettie returning. A man who thought he wasn't needed… A man who wanted to be needed… This could be excellent. She could graciously allow him to unblock her plumbing. She could kindly permit him to push the stroller up the rough part of the track—or maybe she could even suggest if he could rebuild the track.

'Hettie?' He sounded nervous.

'Yes?'

'What are you thinking?'

'Nothing,' she said with insouciance, and suddenly Max

was grinning. He could read her, her Max, and suddenly he was with her, the Max she knew and loved, the Max in charge of his world, who'd returned to take his rightful place as Lockhart of Wildfire.

Her husband.

The father to her son.

'You get to push the stroller,' she said firmly, and he looked astonished.

'What, now?'

'Certainly now. You can push faster than me and we need to go home.'

'I… Yes.' And then he added, still not completely sure, 'Back to the homestead?'

'Certainly. We have work to do.'

'Work?'

'We need to shift those bedrooms,' she said astringently. 'Get all your stuff up to my end of the house, or my stuff up to your end of the house. Depending on whose bed's biggest.'

'Het—'

'And we need to do it before Joni wakes up,' she told him. 'We could make a bed right here but I'm scared of small boys and cameras.'

He choked on joyful laughter, and then, even though speed was imperative, even though his beautiful, bossy Hettie was giving orders he fully intended to comply with, he firmly gathered her into his arms.

'Hettie de Lacey?' he managed and then he kissed her so her answer couldn't come for quite a while.

'Y-yes?' she managed when she came up for air.

'Will you marry me?'

'I thought…I thought I already did.'

'Not properly,' he told her. 'Not the way it ought to be done. I'm a Lockhart of Wildfire and I know what's due to my bride.'

'What?'

'The whole island,' he said in satisfaction, holding her against him, folding her to him so she moulded against his breast, so she felt truly as if she'd found her home. 'We need to repeat our vows in front of every islander, from Wildfire, from the whole of M'Langi if they'll come. Every single islander present, a feast that lasts for days, a celebration to say this is a new beginning. You and me, my love, with Joni and Bugsy and Harry and all our hospital friends and all the islanders... It's a joyous beginning for all of us. I want to work here, Hettie, and I hope I can be needed. I hope together we can make a difference to this place. But we'll do it side by side, my love. As husband and wife. I know you don't need me, but this new system, do you think we could share?'

'It sounds good to me,' she told him, and smiled and smiled. And then she pulled back so she could see him. So she could see all of him, this man she loved with all her heart.

'It sounds wonderful,' she told him. 'Let's start now.'

EPILOGUE

Eighteen months on marked the twenty-fifth anniversary of the opening of the Wildfire hospital. When Ellie had died Max had vowed to get a hospital on the island. It had taken a herculean effort to see it built but now every islander, plus every medic who'd ever worked in the hospital, seemed to be here to celebrate. They were also here to celebrate the new Christopher Lockhart Surgical Wing, built by Harry.

Harry had also funded tonight's *hangi*. It was held on Sunset Beach, below the hospital, and it was a feast to outdo any feast the island had seen before. All day there'd been hospital tours, tours of the new research centre, tours of the amazing new resort, even an underground tour of the now fully operating gold mine. Two years before, Wildfire had been in such financial straits that half the islanders had been unemployed and the hospital threatened with closure. Things couldn't be more different today.

'We've done well.' Harry and Max were standing apart, looking out over the crowd of islanders and medics gathered around the vast fire pit on the beach. Harry gripped Max's shoulder in a gesture of companionship, a gesture that spoke of shared troubles and a similar happy ending. 'This is better than we could ever have hoped,' Harry said in quiet satisfaction, and Max could only agree.

And he wasn't only thinking of the hospital.

Harry's Sarah was helping Hettie build a sandcastle for Joni. At three, Joni was a bossy toddler, happy and self-assured and certain that his way was the right way to get those turrets up, even when they kept falling over. Sarah and Hettie were giggling over the latest disaster, while Joni stomped down to the water's edge with his bucket to get more water.

Both men watched and both men had goofy smiles on their faces.

'We have done well,' Max said softly. 'Thanks to you.'

'Thanks to us,' Harry said firmly. 'Mine was the money. Yours was the persistence and power. Not to mention the encouragement of the two women in our lives.'

'We wouldn't have done it without them,' Max agreed. He tried to change his smile from goofy and failed. Hettie was laughing. Hettie was gorgeous. She was his wife. How could he do anything but smile?

And there was so much more to smile about than the laughter of his lovely wife, he conceded. He had a grandchild now, tiny Christie, born six weeks ago to Caroline and Keanu. Ana and Luke were here, with their daughter, Hana, and their baby, Julien. Sam and Lia were helping Joni scoop up water but Lia was having trouble bending. Eight months into pregnancy, Lia had an excuse not to bend.

And she wouldn't have to go to the mainland to have her baby. That was an amazing source of satisfaction. With the new wing on the hospital and with Harry's funding, they now had a full-time obstetrician on the island, plus an anaesthetist. Max's grandchild had been born on Wildfire with every precaution taken care of.

'And we've not had a single case of encephalitis for the season.' Harry's beam was almost as wide as Max's. 'The trials of the new vaccine seem to have been a resounding success. We can almost rest on our laurels, Dr Lockhart.'

Max grinned back. 'Do you think my Hettie will let me rest? That woman has so many projects...'

'She did tell me you like to be needed,' Harry conceded, smiling across at the doctors in charge of the new clinic out on Atangi. Josh and Maddie and their beautiful baby daughter had come to Wildfire for the celebrations. 'Has she told you her idea for a preschool?'

'No,' Max said, startled, and Harry chuckled.

'I might have known. The elementary school's good but she thinks early schooling's important, especially now we have so many more babies. She's thinking of setting one up on each of the islands and she's already hit me for funding.'

'You've done enough,' Max told him, but Harry shook his head.

'How can I ever have done enough? If I've done enough then I'm not needed. What about you, Max? Have you done enough?'

And Max thought of what he had.

He had enough surgery here to keep him busy full time. He had a wife who loved him. He had a son who came running every time he came into the house, greeting him with joy. He had his daughter and son-in-law and he had a granddaughter who was already promising to be Joni's best friend.

He had friends, he had family, he even had a dog because Hettie decreed that since Maddie had taken Bugsy out to Atangi, there had to be another hospital mascot. Not that Roper was much of a mascot, but the great shaggy cross-bred was certainly a favourite. Max needed to put in a bit of dog training. He had projects to make the M'Langi islands better and better, and Hettie kept thinking up more.

He smiled at her now and she looked up from what she was doing and smiled back, almost as if she could sense he was thinking of her. Her smile was warm, intimate, loving, and it still had the capacity to make his heart turn over.

'What are you plotting?' she called. 'You and Harry?'

'Just what comes next,' he called back, and he couldn't help it. His smile turned goofy again, just like that. 'Just how to be needed for the rest of my life.'

* * * * *

MILLS & BOON®
Hardback – April 2016

ROMANCE

The Sicilian's Stolen Son	Lynne Graham
Seduced into Her Boss's Service	Cathy Williams
The Billionaire's Defiant Acquisition	Sharon Kendrick
One Night to Wedding Vows	Kim Lawrence
Engaged to Her Ravensdale Enemy	Melanie Milburne
A Diamond Deal with the Greek	Maya Blake
Inherited by Ferranti	Kate Hewitt
The Secret to Marrying Marchesi	Amanda Cinelli
The Billionaire's Baby Swap	Rebecca Winters
The Wedding Planner's Big Day	Cara Colter
Holiday with the Best Man	Kate Hardy
Tempted by Her Tycoon Boss	Jennie Adams
Seduced by the Heart Surgeon	Carol Marinelli
Falling for the Single Dad	Emily Forbes
The Fling That Changed Everything	Alison Roberts
A Child to Open Their Hearts	Marion Lennox
The Greek Doctor's Secret Son	Jennifer Taylor
Caught in a Storm of Passion	Lucy Ryder
Take Me, Cowboy	Maisey Yates
His Baby Agenda	Katherine Garbera

MILLS & BOON®
Large Print – April 2016

ROMANCE

The Price of His Redemption	Carol Marinelli
Back in the Brazilian's Bed	Susan Stephens
The Innocent's Sinful Craving	Sara Craven
Brunetti's Secret Son	Maya Blake
Talos Claims His Virgin	Michelle Smart
Destined for the Desert King	Kate Walker
Ravensdale's Defiant Captive	Melanie Milburne
The Best Man & The Wedding Planner	Teresa Carpenter
Proposal at the Winter Ball	Jessica Gilmore
Bodyguard...to Bridegroom?	Nikki Logan
Christmas Kisses with Her Boss	Nina Milne

HISTORICAL

His Christmas Countess	Louise Allen
The Captain's Christmas Bride	Annie Burrows
Lord Lansbury's Christmas Wedding	Helen Dickson
Warrior of Fire	Michelle Willingham
Lady Rowena's Ruin	Carol Townend

MEDICAL

The Baby of Their Dreams	Carol Marinelli
Falling for Her Reluctant Sheikh	Amalie Berlin
Hot-Shot Doc, Secret Dad	Lynne Marshall
Father for Her Newborn Baby	Lynne Marshall
His Little Christmas Miracle	Emily Forbes
Safe in the Surgeon's Arms	Molly Evans

MILLS & BOON®
Hardback – May 2016

ROMANCE

Morelli's Mistress	Anne Mather
A Tycoon to Be Reckoned With	Julia James
Billionaire Without a Past	Carol Marinelli
The Shock Cassano Baby	Andie Brock
The Most Scandalous Ravensdale	Melanie Milburne
The Sheikh's Last Mistress	Rachael Thomas
Claiming the Royal Innocent	Jennifer Hayward
Kept at the Argentine's Command	Lucy Ellis
The Billionaire Who Saw Her Beauty	Rebecca Winters
In the Boss's Castle	Jessica Gilmore
One Week with the French Tycoon	Christy McKellen
Rafael's Contract Bride	Nina Milne
Tempted by Hollywood's Top Doc	Louisa George
Perfect Rivals...	Amy Ruttan
English Rose in the Outback	Lucy Clark
A Family for Chloe	Lucy Clark
The Doctor's Baby Secret	Scarlet Wilson
Married for the Boss's Baby	Susan Carlisle
Twins for the Texan	Charlene Sands
Secret Baby Scandal	Joanne Rock

MILLS & BOON®
Large Print – May 2016

ROMANCE

The Queen's New Year Secret	Maisey Yates
Wearing the De Angelis Ring	Cathy Williams
The Cost of the Forbidden	Carol Marinelli
Mistress of His Revenge	Chantelle Shaw
Theseus Discovers His Heir	Michelle Smart
The Marriage He Must Keep	Dani Collins
Awakening the Ravensdale Heiress	Melanie Milburne
His Princess of Convenience	Rebecca Winters
Holiday with the Millionaire	Scarlet Wilson
The Husband She'd Never Met	Barbara Hannay
Unlocking Her Boss's Heart	Christy McKellen

HISTORICAL

In Debt to the Earl	Elizabeth Rolls
Rake Most Likely to Seduce	Bronwyn Scott
The Captain and His Innocent	Lucy Ashford
Scoundrel of Dunborough	Margaret Moore
One Night with the Viking	Harper St. George

MEDICAL

A Touch of Christmas Magic	Scarlet Wilson
Her Christmas Baby Bump	Robin Gianna
Winter Wedding in Vegas	Janice Lynn
One Night Before Christmas	Susan Carlisle
A December to Remember	Sue MacKay
A Father This Christmas?	Louisa Heaton

MILLS & BOON®

Why shop at millsandboon.co.uk?

Each year, thousands of romance readers find their perfect read at millsandboon.co.uk. That's because we're passionate about bringing you the very best romantic fiction. Here are some of the advantages of shopping at www.millsandboon.co.uk:

* **Get new books first**—you'll be able to buy your favourite books one month before they hit the shops

* **Get exclusive discounts**—you'll also be able to buy our specially created monthly collections, with up to 50% off the RRP

* **Find your favourite authors**—latest news, interviews and new releases for all your favourite authors and series on our website, plus ideas for what to try next

* **Join in**—once you've bought your favourite books, don't forget to register with us to rate, review and join in the discussions

Visit **www.millsandboon.co.uk**
for all this and more today!